J. D. WILLIAMS

Bound by Song

This book was professionally typeset on Reedsy.
Find out more at reedsy.com

Contents

About Bound by Song

Singer-songwriter Julia Tate moved out of Nashville to get away from successful music producer Raine Wagner, who was the love of her life until he broke her heart into a million little pieces.

Bound by Song, the first book in the Julia Tate Song Series, rekindles the romance between two heartsick souls, Julia and Raine, as a new music reality show fatefully draws them back into each other's lives. Will their love affair destroy her musical dream?

Julia Tate Song Series

Bound by Song leads book two, *Born by Song*, and the final book, *Blessed by Song*, through the popular music industry as Julia Tate becomes a beloved singer-songwriter against all the odds, inspiring millions of fans. Julia strikes a powerful chord as she encourages women to follow their own dreams of career, motherhood, and love. The background world of music is positively intertwined throughout the books, adding to the allure of celebrity, while giving real insight into the challenging world of the music industry.

Born by Song coming in January of 2024. *Blessed by Song* coming in 2024.

For more information, go to www.jdwilliamsbooks.com

Acknowledgments

Thank you, Jill, and Sydney for reviewing covers, creative, and providing feedback. Thank you to my two great editors for their insight and expertise. Thanks to Artillery Media for doing such a wonderful, creative job on the website. Also, thanks to those who have been so supportive with your kind messages and words of encouragement about the corresponding music (Pamela, Kim, Roxann, Travis, Ron, Jill C., Ken, and Scott) and all those who have liked, shared, and streamed songs.

Lastly, a special thanks to my dad and all my family, and thank you to Chris, for putting up with the process and supporting me every step of the way.

Chapter One - Julia

When I finally let go of my death grip on the steering wheel, I have leather groove marks on my hands. Some days, gripping the steering wheel of my old Jeep is the only thing I have left. I gave up my old life back in Nashville: my love of music, my dream of writing songs, and the love of my life, Raine Wagner. Raine destroyed me, and in the process, my love of anything that had to do with music.

But now, I'm facing a second chance at my first love. I sent an audition tape in for the new reality show *Next Real Star*, and they contacted me for a live audition for some of the show's producers. The one thing I really like about this new reality show is each contestant has to sing a song he or she has written. Since no song covers are allowed, it really puts an emphasis on writing, not just performing.

As I sit outside of a large arena in Kansas City, three hours from my hometown in Nebraska, I try to steel myself to walk inside, but my legs are glued to the worn leather seats. It's safe here, and I like safe. I am terrified to walk into that building, but here I am trying to overcome years of doubt and stage fright to give it one last shot. I hope to prove not only to myself that I can do it, but to anyone who ever told me that I would never make it as a singer-songwriter or made me feel like I was not enough. And the first person on that list is Raine.

I let out a long, heavy sigh. "Just breathe," I say to myself as I glance in the rear-view mirror at my wide-eyed reflection staring back. "It's now or never. This is your *last* chance."

I get out, open the back door, grab my guitar and my bag with my outfit and makeup. Today, I'll sing with the show's live band. My heart is giving a runaway freight train a run for its money. In fact, I wonder if people can see it beating through my now sweat-soaked shirt. I pull my shoulders back and toss my long hair away from my flushed face as I walk toward the big, heavy metal doors of the arena, wondering if a firing squad will meet me on the other side. Once inside, I approach a table by the front entrance.

"Name?"

"Julia Tate."

"Ms. Tate, you're number twenty-four out of thirty singers today. Be prepared to sing two different songs, but you probably won't get through each song. Dressing rooms are down the hall to your left. You're welcome to listen to the others auditioning. Good luck," the young show rep says without ever really looking at me, and when she finally does, she gives me a smile that doesn't quite reach her eyes.

"Thanks, I'll need it," I joke, but the rep looks over my head, gesturing toward a young man waiting behind me.

As I walk into the dressing room to get ready, I'm struck by the youth of the other contestants. Only one other person looks close to my age, and I'm not sure if the woman is someone's mother or another contestant. I try to maintain my confidence as I walk in the room, but it's hard not to notice when you are the oldest person in the room, and I can't help but wonder if I'm about to make a complete fool of myself. "Here we go, God. I need you on this one," I mutter under my breath.

About an hour later, a stagehand walks up and loudly calls out, "Number twenty-four!"

I've been waiting backstage with my earbuds in. I don't want to listen to the other contestants; it will make my nerves even more frayed. I asked a stagehand to let me know when I was up, and he's frantically waving at me. I cram my earbuds in my bag, stand, and smooth out my dress while checking my face in the mirror one last time. As I leave the room, I tighten the grip on my guitar, and boldly stride toward the stage. But inside, my stomach is doing somersaults, and acid is slowly rising in my throat, ready to make its own appearance. I'm pretty sure I'm going to vomit. It's happened before.

2

When I hit the stage, I look out toward the mostly empty arena and smile, but my upper lip is doing a little nervous twitch of its own and I wonder if anyone can see it. I'm wearing a long red gown, which I'd been told is a good color with my dark hair and blue eyes. I purposely didn't want the typical "country singer wearing a short dress and boots" look. At forty, I have to pull out all the stops to get on a show like this, so I went for a look that is more Golden Globes. I head toward the lone microphone stand in the middle of the stage, grab the cord, and plug in my guitar. As I look out toward the audience, the lights are blinding. Again, my stomach flip-flops. I silently pray, *please, don't let me throw up.*

I'm put through the drill again.

"Name?" an uninterested, faceless voice asks from the concert hall.

I squint out at the silhouettes, seated behind a table at the front. "Julia Tate," I say, clearing my tightly constricted throat. How will I ever get through this?

"All right, when you're ready."

I pause for what feels like a lifetime, pull the pick from out of my guitar's fret board, and strum a few chords. My fingers are shaking, but I still manage to make the chords sing. I had given chord charts to the band, and I glance back at them, nod, and then count off and start playing. I take a deep and ragged breath and open my mouth, letting the notes fly out. At first, my voice is shaky but soon I hit my stride.

There is a loud, restless rumbling from the small crowd, but after a few seconds, the audience is silent. I can hear my voice echo through the near-empty hall. I know, like I've known and felt many times before, that when you're doing what you are meant to do at exactly the right time, something amazing happens. It's a spiritual, out-of-body experience, like God is turning on his light at that moment and helping you out. I sing the chorus, *"The end's harder than you think, comes on stronger than you know. Goodbye rushes toward you. There won't be … a tomorrow."*

My words are about losing the love of my life and a painful goodbye, and I give each note a level of emotion I've kept contained for months. Surprisingly, they let me sing the entire song, and as I hit the last chord on my guitar, the small crowd of contestants and a few stagehands are clapping and cheering. It brings a smile to my lips, which have finally stopped quivering. I squint toward the silent table, waiting for the almighty producers to decide my fate.

After a few seconds, I hear a man's deep voice, "Julia, how old are you?"

My mouth instantly goes dry. The dreaded question I knew would come. "I turned forty a few months ago," I reply.

"Right." A long pause, and all I can hear are mumblings from the table. A couple of audience members yell out for me to sing another.

Finally, a woman speaks from the table, "Julia, we don't need to hear another, we're good."

I give a nod and start to pull the chord from the guitar, holding it up toward the soundboard to let them know. I calmly try to keep my composure as I make my way to the side of the stage. Thankfully, a few audience members are still clapping, so I wave back at them. In my mind, I'm already replaying the scene, wondering if I blew it, but at least a couple of people are clapping. Right now, and at my age, this feels great, but they only let me sing one song. One song. Not a good sign.

These auditions are a crap shoot, but for the first time in many years, I'm proud of myself, and my grin is as big as the Cheshire cat as I walk toward the dressing room to change. I don't have a clue if I will make it through and end up on the show in Vegas. No matter what, by facing my fears and auditioning, I've already won.

Chapter Two – Julia

As I drive home, I can't get my mind off one man: Raine Wagner. I can vividly picture him standing in front of me. Tall, with dark, spiky hair he purposely messes up that makes him look cool. Green, slightly hazel eyes that with one look, would peer into my soul. Coupled with the sly grin that basically never leaves his face, it's as if he knew all my secrets, and then he'd say something that made me think he was reading my mind.

I met Raine while living in Nashville. Early on, Raine was a struggling but amazing guitarist. Now he's a successful music producer, songwriter, and musician. His songs are some of the biggest hits on country radio, and he works with one of the hottest country superstars, Bret Savage. I always knew Raine would be successful. He's the most driven and talented person I've ever known, but unfortunately, also an arrogant, cheating asshole.

"Ugh!" I exclaim loudly as I twist in my seat, trying to shake my memories of his face and every aspect of his firm, lean body from my mind. I didn't want to go down this soul-draining path. Damn! And then my mind goes there. Best. Sex. Ever. I had never had better, and I doubt I ever will. A vivid image of Raine towering over me in a state of undress flashes before my eyes. "I have got to get him out of my mind!" I say out loud.

There is only one person to help, and that's my best friend, Tracy. When I'm in a dark place thinking about Raine, she always lightens up the mood. She is bubbly, witty, and the most forward person I've ever met. At the very least, she'll distract me. Tracy picks up after a couple of rings.

There are no formal salutations. "How'd it go? Do you know if you are moving on?" Tracy asks, barely bothering to pause for a breath.

"I think it went well, but really, no idea," I'm able to squeeze into the conversation before she cuts me off.

"That's ridiculous! Well, when will you find out?"

"If you give me a chance, girlfriend, I'll tell you everything I know," I say with a laugh. Tracy laughs as well, and I'm able to let her know how it went.

"I think it went better than you think. You always tend to think the worst," she says.

I hope she's right, but I've had too many near-misses in the music business, and I've learned not to get my hopes up. There's only so much music career heartbreak one person can bear. "But like I said, only one song. I didn't vomit though, and the crowd seemed to like it, yada, yada, yada."

"We'll see, so what else is going on? This has to do with Raine, doesn't it? You haven't really thought about music for years, and now this. What's up?"

She knows me too well. "Well, you nailed it. It doesn't help that one of Raine's songs is always on the damn radio," I say with a laugh.

"No, I suppose it doesn't," she says, and after a slight pause, she asks, "If you make it on the show, are you going to call him, just to let him know?"

"No way in hell. If I'm lucky enough to make it on the show, he can find out on the ol' television, just like everyone else." But it's the first time I've really thought about it. What if I do make it on the show? I would want him to know, wouldn't I?

"Jules, I know he broke your heart in a million little pieces but at one time, you were close. I'm sure he misses you, and I know if he found out you were on the show, he'd want you to do well."

"Nope, that ship has sailed. He never chose me, Tracy. Ever. He always chose someone else over me, and that last time was a doozy. Remember Bethany? The young, blonde backup singer I found him in bed with. Nope. No way, no how."

"Okey dokey," she says in her strong northern accent. "If you do end up going to Vegas for the show, I'm going with you. We would tear up that town!"

"Of that, I have no doubt," I say, laughing as the call ends.

Although Tracy has helped distract my mind, she often weaves Raine into our conversations. She's his friend too. The good thing is that it makes me remember how much shit that man put me through.

I turn the radio back on just as a familiar song plays. It never fails. Raine recently wrote and produced the song for Bret. My throat constricts and my insides turn. Why? Why does the radio and everything around me remind me of Raine? It seems at every turn, I'll hear one of his songs or see a tall man with black hair, and suddenly the memories flood in. Is it because I'm always looking for his face in a crowd? Even though I moved eight hundred miles away to avoid him, there he is in my head and my heart, never letting me go.

I listen to Raine's song. It's about the regrets and mistakes we make in life that alter our course. I've followed his career for the past few years and know most of the songs he's written and the artists he's producing. After I left Nashville, Raine's success grew rapidly, which doesn't seem fair. He hurt me, so he doesn't deserve fortune and happiness. After what he did, he just doesn't deserve it.

I think about my love for music. A love I shared with Raine. The difference is that Raine is living his dream, and I walked away. No, I *ran* away from my dream. For many years I blamed Raine, but deep down I know it's my fault. I didn't fight hard enough or long enough for what I wanted.

I had given up writing music and performing, but now here I am driving away from an audition that could change my life and give me everything I'd ever dreamed of. After all this time, I'm singing and writing again. Even if I don't make it on the show, I didn't give up.

I reach down and turn up the volume. My chest tightens as I wonder if hearing Raine's song is a sign. I glance at my phone, picking it up as I've done so many times, and almost call him, but I turn my phone off. I won't. I shake my head trying to clear the memories. God, I miss him and deep down, I know I'll always love him, but Raine will never love me, at least not in the same way. I was never enough. I have to let him go. I just wish my mind could convince my heart.

Chapter Three – Raine

It takes something incredibly serious to get me to wear a suit in the middle of the day. I'm sitting in a conference room chair, leaning against the table with my arms crossed in front of me, staring at the TV executives. The execs traveled to Nashville to meet with me and my lawyer, offering me a spot as a judge on the new reality show *Next Real Star*. I know my reputation is part of the reason. I'm known for being incredibly straightforward. I've even heard the word "asshole" more than once under someone's breath, but I'm incredibly driven and all my acts, to this point, are successful because I won't let them fail. Yes, I may be an asshole, but I'm a successful asshole, so I'll take it. The show will take me away from producing, but I need the exposure right now. Things have stalled a bit, and the show will propel my career to an even higher level.

The TV execs and their lawyers continue to hash out the details with my lawyer, but in my head, it's a done deal. I'm not sure why I'm here in the room as I tap my pen on the table, listening to the others drone on, watching the conversation as if I'm at a tennis match. I don't sit still well, and all I can think about is Julia. Julia Tate. I let her get away years ago, and now all I want is for her to know I'll be a celebrity judge. Maybe in some strange way, by seeing me on the show, it will make her want to contact me and I can convince her that I'm a better man. I know that now. But in my heart, I know why she left and refuses to talk to me. I messed up in a big way, and she'll never give me another chance.

My stomach turns thinking of how I hurt her over and over again. Julia hates my guts, and I deserve it. But if there is any chance that deep inside her heart she misses me, I have to try. Julia never leaves my mind, no matter how many other women I've slept with or how much I drink. No matter how hard I've tried to forget, she is always there, haunting my thoughts and stirring up memories.

The conversation between the TV execs and lawyers finally ends, and it brings me out of my reverie.

"The first show will be in Vegas the same week as the Academy of Country Music Awards in April," a vice president rattles off. "We'll introduce Raine, seated at the judges' table for the first live show. We'll have eliminated contestants and we'll be down to the final twenty performers at that point."

I look at my lawyer and nod.

"Sounds like we are in," my lawyer replies.

My thoughts instantly flash to Julia. National TV. She'll have to see me on the show, she won't be able to miss it.

##

As I slide my tall frame into my truck, I grab my cell phone and call Bret Savage. Bret is my only confidant, and if anyone can help get me out of this Julia funk, he can. And that's all this is, a funk. I want someone I can't have, someone out of my reach.

"So, I hear you're the next big rock star reality show judge," Bret says, laughing sarcastically.

"How in the hell would you know about that?" I reply.

"Buddy, I have people everywhere and they tell me everything. There have been rumors about a new show, and frankly you're not as slick as you think," he drawls in his strong Texas accent.

"Right. Well … I know nothing," I say, as if I'm being covert. "Except that I just might be in Vegas at the same time as the Academy of Country Music awards. Since you'll be there too, we need to plan some R&R. I need it."

"You got that right. Great golf in that town."

"How about my people get with your people?" I say, sarcasm oozing with every syllable.

"I'll get right on that," Bret replies as he hangs up.

I smile to myself. I can always count on Bret. As I start my Ford F-250 and roll out of the parking garage, I'm struck with a strong sense of longing for a different time, or maybe it's different choices. I'd give anything to see Julia again.

"I wonder if she even thinks about me," I say out loud.

And then I'm lost in memories. Julia in a skin-tight red dress, her bright blue eyes dancing, laughing at something I said during dinner. God, she had a great laugh. Strong and abrupt but light at the same time. I can picture her in my bed, her dark hair covering me as she leans in to kiss me. My face is now glistening with sweat as I twitch uncomfortably.

A car horn takes me out of my daydream, and I realize the light has turned green. *Damn!* When will Julia leave my mind and give me some peace? Sometimes, I think it will never happen. Her loss is like a heavy coat I carry, weighing me down.

As I drive, I remember the last time I sent her a text asking to speak with her, but she refused. It was a year after she had found me in bed with that background singer, Bethany. I was such an idiot. I tried to reach out to her when I heard she had a new, guitar-player boyfriend. The thought of Julia with another man makes me sick to my stomach. Now I don't know where she is, but I hope she's happy.

I run my hand through my dark hair and sigh. For more than two years, I had no word from or about her. As much as I try not to care, I do care deeply. No one, not one woman, understood me like she did. Julia could always deal with my insane drive and idiosyncrasies, and she loves music as much as, if not more than, I do. I didn't think anyone could love music more than me. Music is air to me. Julia also lived and breathed lyrics and the art of transforming three minutes into a story that touches people. If I could just get one chance to talk to her and make her see how much I've changed, I'd take it.

"What's the use," I say out loud. Julia's gone. That's it. She's gone, and who am I kidding? She'll never come back to me.

Chapter Four – Julia

"The show just called. I did it!" I practically shriek to Tracy over the phone, pacing around my living room, the excitement of my words resonating with every step. "I'm in the top twenty. Can you believe it?! Oh my God … I have no idea what I'm going to sing, or wear for that matter," I say, collapsing on my couch.

"I'm so glad you auditioned," Tracy replies with excitement. "Dang girl, I am so proud of you! So, what happens next?"

"Well, first, I have to get out of work, but in about two weeks, I fly out to Vegas for the first live show, which is the same week as the ACM awards. The show's producers won't tell me much, just where to be and when. I can bring one family member or friend. So, if you're still game, the invite's open. I'm not sure Vegas can handle both of us at the same time though," I say jokingly. My fun-filled history with Tracy is infamous.

Tracy's bubbly enthusiasm continues, "That's perfect! I have some vacation saved up, and it shouldn't be a problem to come out for a few days. This is going to be great!"

"You know, I'm probably the only female contestant over the age of forty. I'm a long shot, but at least I made it."

"They're lucky to have you. Do you know who the judges are going to be?"

"No, not a clue, they're keeping it a secret until the first show. I won't know who any of the judges or contestants will be, I just hope they're open-minded to someone my age."

"It should only be about talent, and you've got that covered." Tracy pauses for a moment before continuing, "You do realize Raine will probably be in

Vegas for the ACMs. You'll run into him … you always do."

"That thought had crossed my mind," I say as my voice cracks. I'm sure Tracy hears.

"What would you do?"

"Throw a drink in his face," I say without hesitation, but my stomach turns. Although part of me wants Raine to rot in hell forever, another part of me wants to see him. I can't help it. After all this time and all that man put me through, my feelings for him never seem to go away.

Tracy replies, "I personally cannot wait for him to find out you're a contestant on the show. You can show him you've moved on. And then when you win, you can tell him exactly where to go, and work with another producer."

"You're right, I could," I say with more bravado than I feel. I still have a soft spot for Raine. I'll talk a big game, but purposefully hurting him is not on my agenda.

When I end the call with Tracy, I realize all this talk about the show and Raine has frayed my already fragile nerves. I head into the kitchen to pour a glass of red wine. I walk over and sit on my living room couch, staring out the window at a clear night sky, the glass of wine in my hand. The moon is full and bright, and it reminds me of the first night I was out with Raine so many years ago. It was an outdoor concert in downtown Nashville, and I can picture the scene like it was yesterday.

I was standing at the edge of the crowd. I went to the show by myself and didn't know anyone there, so I just hung back and listened. I'd met Raine a few days before and he mentioned the show and asked if I planned on going. It seemed like an invitation, and I didn't have anything going on that night, so I went. I was about to leave when I turned around and there he was, as if waiting for me. I can still picture him walking up with a purposeful look full of strength and safety. Maybe it was how he was walking directly toward me that made me fall in love with him right at that moment.

We spent the evening hanging out and listening to live music. The connection between us was instant and comfortable, like we'd been together for years. I remember how he pulled me tight against his body and kissed me hard on the lips, his strong arms engulfing me as he held me tight against his firm chest. Raine was confident and captured attention wherever he went. He was the kind of person who took charge, and I liked that about him.

For the first few months, we'd sit and talk about artists and songs for hours. Ever since I was a little girl, music had been my saving grace. Raised by a single father, I spent many hours alone while my dad was at work, and music was often all I had. From the time I was little, writing and recording music had been my dream. I loved being on stage. It was the only place I truly felt comfortable. It has a warmth, and the love from an audience … there is nothing else like it.

I dated Raine off and on for years. We broke up the first time because Raine's career consumed him, and I always took a back seat to everything. It finally became too much for me, and I broke up with him to date someone else, but I kept running into Raine. Then we would try to date again but he would eventually fade away and date someone else. But we would just happen to run into each other, and the affair would all start over again. Raine had a way of pulling me back in, even when I knew it was a big mistake.

Our relationship was always tumultuous. Raine always seemed to be searching for someone else. I wouldn't say looking for someone better, I have too much respect for myself. But Raine's shallow and likely wanted someone new. Whatever. When he couldn't find anyone else who understood him, he'd come looking for me. We had a passionate and reckless relationship that had finally ended badly.

I can't remember how many times we dated and then it would end, but for many years, it happened a lot. Too many times. Until the one night I caught him with that girl, and it changed everything. I can still vividly picture him in bed with Bethany. In my heart I knew I would never be enough for him. I was finally done.

##

Two weeks later I wake up in bed, drenched in sweat. I had the same nightmare. The nightmare I've had for years whenever I'm thinking a lot about Raine. It always starts with the night I found Raine in bed with Bethany.

Raine had given me a key to his house, and one night, I'd let myself in to surprise him. As I entered the house, it was quiet. Too quiet. There were liquor bottles and glasses strewn all over the kitchen counters. Obviously, he had a party, which was common with his musician and writer friends who would show up for a drink, or ten.

In my dream, Raine has left the stereo on, and I can vaguely pick out a Sting song playing in the background. I walk through the house toward the steps that lead up to his bedroom, and my body is instantly heavy, filled with dread, like I'm walking in sand, but I push on and continue walking up the stairs. The hairs on the back of my neck go up and I'm suffocating. My legs are heavy like tree trunks, and my breath is labored. Just as I'm about to open his bedroom door, I wake up. Every single time, I wake up at this same point in the dream.

In reality when I opened Raine's bedroom door, he was lying naked on his bed as Bethany leaned over him, kissing him. Raine had used this same background singer on many of his projects. Bethany had always been a bitch to me, and that night, I discovered why.

I lean up in my bed and wipe the sweat off my brow. How one man could cause me so much turmoil is beyond comprehension. That night, I stormed out of Raine's house and drove home in a tear-streaked fog. When I got home, I left a message on his voicemail, more pissed at myself than anything. I'd let his behavior go on for far too long. Thinking about it now makes my head hurt.

After finding Raine with Bethany that night, I asked him to leave me alone, and for the most part he did. He only tried to contact me once after that night. It was like he just dropped off the face of the earth, and deep down I don't know which hurts worse, the fact that he cheated on me, or that he never even tried to explain it. It's like I didn't mean anything to him at all.

I drag myself out of bed and pull on an old T-shirt with *The Doors* across the front and stagger to the kitchen to make coffee. Why did I ever let myself fall in love with Raine? Why didn't I know he was cheating, and how long had it been going on? Why did I let him treat me that way? I absentmindedly put my hands to my temples, trying to rub him out of my mind. Some days

I'm drowning in regret, and I don't think it will ever go away. I've made so many mistakes, but the biggest mistake was falling in love with that man.

I pour myself some much-needed coffee and stare out the back kitchen window. Since Raine, I've never really trusted anyone. Oh, I still date. Young guys, old guys, and even a couple of ex-boyfriends, but I've never been able to give my heart to anyone else, at least not yet. I still hold out hope I'll get that S.O.B. out of my mind and out of my blood. He's like a drug, and my body aches from missing him and needing another fix.

Tracy sends me a text and brings me out of my misery. 'Your flight leaves tomorrow, right? I'll be there shortly after you ... can't wait!! Party!!'

I text back, 'Girl, you have no idea how excited I am to see you and get this show on the road. On to the next, best chapter, ever!'

I put my phone back down and stare back out the kitchen window, drinking my coffee and trying to focus on the upcoming reality show. This is my second chance. I desperately need this fresh start, and that should be my focus, nothing else. Not Raine, not regrets, not anything else but singing, writing, and doing well on this show. I think about the first song I'll sing on the show, and in hindsight, maybe leaving Nashville was the best thing that ever happened to me? I'm writing more songs than I have in years, and I'm a much stronger person. I have a new life and I'm clearing my head from all the debris of sad Raine memories.

Raine was my muse, and now he's the nemesis I often use in my song lyrics. He's a big part of why I stuck my neck out and auditioned for the show. I want to prove him wrong and show him that I didn't give up. I want him to know I can move on, and I want him to want what he'll never have again. Now is the time to open my heart to new memories and put *me* first. I just have one obstacle: the pesky problem of getting Raine out of my head and heart once and for all.

Chapter Five – Raine

I'm sitting in my home office on the phone with one of the show's producers as she explains the upcoming schedule for the first live *Next Real Star* show.

"So, I just need to be in Vegas ready to go for the first night's live show, no other appearances before that?" I ask.

"Correct," she replies. "You won't have to do any press or anything before the first live show. Contestants and judges will be introduced that first night. All contestant songs are originals, and the contestants are graded by the judges on the quality of their song and performance."

"Sounds good. I'll be there a few days early for the ACMs and interviews with Bret, so I'm available if you need anything."

I hang up the phone and smile to myself. I need some fun in Vegas before the real work begins. It'll help clear my mind to hang with Bret, who's always up for a good time, and we've had plenty. Maybe I'll meet someone new, but that thought quickly fades as my mind drifts to Julia. I rub my brow trying to clear her from my thoughts, but there she is again, drifting in and out of my mind. I have no control over it. She is always there, haunting my thoughts and memories.

I toy with an idea of how to casually let Julia know about my new show. But it's no use, I'm bound to secrecy.

"*Fuck. Fuck. Fuck,*" I say as I pace around my office. Maybe Bret will tell Julia? They're casual friends, and he could just text her about it. Wait, what the hell am I thinking? Although Bret knows Julia, he hasn't talked to her in years. Julia would know something is up. I just need one chance to tell her the truth and show her I'm not the man I was years ago. No longer am I the thoughtless, uncaring asshole I was before, at least not privately. Publicly and professionally maybe, but that's different. Now, I would never take Julia for granted. Not anymore. I know how it feels to lose and lose big. Losing her changed everything. I let the best thing that ever came into my life go without a fight, and I'm living with that regret.

I sigh and pick up my phone. No messages from Bret or anyone. It's going to be a long night. I walk into my kitchen and pour a glass of bourbon. I hold the glass in one hand and the bottle of bourbon in the other as I aimlessly walk around my silent home, pausing at memories of Julia in every room. We made love on the leather couch once. I can picture myself sitting there watching Julia undress, her silhouette lit by the fireplace. She straddled me completely nude except for stiletto platforms. My fingers tingle as I remember gripping her waist, watching her use me for pleasure. I can still see her face, hear her voice, and almost smell her perfume. I can picture myself taking her by the hand and leading her to my bedroom.

Tonight, I can't face that same bedroom. She'll stalk me everywhere in that room. I slouch in a leather chair and turn on the flat screen, flipping through a few channels and finally settling on something mindless. But as I glance at my couch, I swear I can see her naked, beautiful body. What I wouldn't give to be in that moment right now.

"*DAMN IT!*" I say out loud.

I know I'm the reason Julia will never give me another chance, let alone speak to me. She gave up on me after that night with Bethany. I don't clearly remember what happened. I only remember the voicemail Julia left after seeing me with another woman. How could I have been so stupid? It was obvious Bethany had been after me for months, but I'd ignored it, thinking she would finally get the hint. I thought I could handle it, but I didn't. I failed Julia. I failed her many times, and it was my stupidity that made her walk away for good.

I pick up the bottle of bourbon and pour the mind-numbing liquid to the top of my glass. I reach down and again pick up my phone. Still no messages. It's definitely going to be a long night.

Chapter Six – Raine

I'm frantically packing up last-minute items in my suitcase when the phone rings. It's Bret, who's probably already set up a round at the golf course right when I land. There are only two things Bret cares about right now and that's music and golf, and golf is probably at the top.

"Hey buddy, you headin' out tomorrow?" Bret asks.

"Yep, in the morning," I say, my voice lacking any enthusiasm for this trip and the new show opportunity.

"You sound absolutely thrilled," Bret drawls before continuing, "Have you tried to reach her ... just send Julia a text."

Even Bret knows I'm still in love with Julia. "She said don't contact her, so I won't. She doesn't want to talk to me, you know that. Nope. And who knows, she's probably married or something."

"Raine, Julia needs to know the truth. I know you, and you have been an absolute drag to hang out with these past few months, shit, if not years. It's been a long time. People change. You could at least try?"

"If she wants to talk to me ... what am I thinking? If by some random chance she even remembers my name, then it is up to her," I say without conviction, knowing if I did get a chance, I'd jump at it.

"All right ... all right. I'll be in Vegas in a day, and I've already got reservations at our favorite course. You better be ready."

I end the call, hanging up disgusted with myself, but maybe Bret is right. It's been a few years. Some of her venom must have dissipated by now, shouldn't it have? But pride keeps me from trying to reach her. It's odd though. Julia is like a sixth sense, and I'm thinking about her more now than ever.

I finish packing, getting everything just right, and then I fill a glass of bourbon, and walk out on my patio. I sit down on one of my loungers and light a cigar, putting my feet up on a table. Music is blaring through my speakers but I'm not paying attention to what's playing. It's melancholy and fits my mood. I can clearly see every star in the sky. I keep getting up and pacing around the patio full of my high-strung energy.

I just finished producing a project for a new female artist, and I'm about to start on Bret's fourth album. Everything is going well, and with this new show, I think it will bolster my schedule. I have success and the lifestyle I've always wanted. I can do what I want, when I want, and I don't have to answer to anyone, but I'm empty. I don't have anyone to share my success with. And not just anyone, I don't have her. Julia's like a tattoo I love but every time I see it, I want to rub the constant reminder off my skin. That's what Julia has done to me. Left my heart with a permanent mark I can't erase. I'm lost.

I drop heavily into a patio chair and swirl my glass of bourbon. I bet she never gives me a second thought. I look up at the night sky and wonder where she is. I take another drink, lingering on memories, remembering her touch, missing the way she'd curl up next to me at night while we slept. Memories of watching her sleep haunt me. If I could just hold her one more time.

I take a drag off my cigar, watching the smoke curl upward and the wind carry it away. I take another long drink, lean back into the chair, and stare at the near empty glass. On nights like this, bourbon is my best friend.

Chapter Seven – Julia

My plane lands in Vegas. I collect my bags and make my way to my waiting car, trying to calm myself down. After all these years, I still can't believe I'm going to sing live, and the nerves are already kicking in.

During the past two weeks, I've been exercising nonstop and preparing for the show. I've brought several new dresses, outfits, and my favorite thing, new shoes. Back home, I had exercise to keep the stress and anxiety at bay, but right now, anxiety is rearing its ugly head, and I think stomach acid will be my constant companion.

"*Holy crap*," I say out loud as I slide my sweaty hands down my jeans. My driver glances at me through the rear-view. I just nod at him. He must think I'm losing my mind. It'll help when Tracy arrives. She has a way of calming me down.

I arrive at the hotel, change into something comfortable, and settle into my room, but I'm pacing around, flipping the television off and on, and glancing at my phone until finally I decide I've got to do something to keep my mind busy. So, shopping it is. Not that I need to spend the money, but I've got to do something.

As I walk through the hotel lobby, my mind drifts to Raine. Knowing he's probably here in Vegas for the ACMs has me scanning the crowd. I wonder what he would think about me being on *Next Real Star* and finally following my dream. He'd probably shit, I think with a smile. A lady passes by and looks at me like I've lost it. Okay, I need to cut back on the crazy and keep everything in check, I think chuckling. No more thoughts about "he-who-shall-not-be-named."

Earlier today, I talked with my sister Jody, letting her know I'd arrived safely. The show's producers realized that contestants needed to tell some family about the show in case of an emergency, and for obvious safety reasons.

Jody knows about my battle with stage fright and encouraged me to get a massage or pedicure or something, and right now, I think she's right. I've got to do something to take the edge off. Maybe my own special spa day will do the trick. I also talked with Jody about how she'll tell the rest of the family to watch *Next Real Star* without giving away any details. I'm sure everyone will think something is up, but I can count on Jody to keep the secret.

About an hour later, Tracy arrives. Finally. I couldn't take much more of the aimless wandering around Vegas.

That night, we make reservations for dinner at a trendy upscale restaurant. Tracy wants to celebrate a bit and I can't turn her down. Plus, it'll be fun to get dressed up for a night on the town before all the hoopla starts.

We dress for dinner and catch an Uber from our hotel to the restaurant. As we slowly snake down the streets of Vegas, I scan the streets for Raine. I can't help it. It's like I can feel he's in the same city, close to me.

Tracy says, "He won't be hard to miss, if he's here."

She knows me too well. "Yes, he would tower over most people in the crowd," I say, giving her a sideways glance. "If Bret is with him, they'll be easy to spot. Bret will have dozens of young girls following him around and screaming," I joke.

"True. Bret does usually attract a lot of female attention, not only because he's famous but that man is gorgeous," she says with a big smile and roll of her eyes. Tracy has a thing for the *GQ* type, whereas I prefer someone a bit more rugged, with an edge … like Raine. Tracy continues, "And what was it you were going to do if you see Raine?"

"Kick him in the balls … no wait, it was something about a drink," I say with a mischievous grin. "Okay, maybe too violent," I reply with a grunt, followed with a laugh. She laughs too. I pause slightly before turning serious. "Honestly, I don't know. You'd think I'd be over him, but I'm not. In a twisted way, I want to see him."

21

"How about I douse him with a drink then?"

"Sounds good," I say, laughing. "I'll be ready to capture it on my phone." I can always count on Tracy to get my twisted sense of humor and have my back.

We enter the restaurant, and they seat us in the upper area. We are tucked away from the main floor but have a good view of the entire dining room. I sit with my back to the entrance. Tracy is sitting directly across from me, with her chair facing the front entrance.

We order a bottle of wine and an appetizer, and right after the server drops them off at our table, Tracy glances toward the front of the restaurant and gasps out loud, her eyes wide, as her hand instantly goes to her mouth. I quickly look at her, and then turn my head to follow her eyes, which are staring at the entrance. Raine is standing at the entrance, talking to the hostess, and then he glances down at his cell phone.

I can't breathe … even though he's across the room, he looks good. Too good. Damn him. He's dressed to kill in a black suit and tie, with his signature dark, slightly mussed hair. He is towering over the hostess and most people around him. Just then, Bret Savage, also immaculately dressed, walks in with his security in tow and slaps Raine on the shoulder. I watch the two of them greet each other, frozen to my chair. Of all the restaurants in Vegas, he shows up at this one. For fuck's sake.

I watch as the hostess leads Raine and Bret to a room just off the entrance. I whirl back around, and Tracy and I stare at each other, wide-eyed. In the back of my mind, I had hoped to run into Raine, but not yet. I realize it's too soon. I'm not ready to face the man who wrecked me years ago. I pick up my glass of Chardonnay, down it, and fidget with my napkin, my eyes darting to Tracy, and then back to the room Raine's in. Tracy looks at me sympathetically.

"I don't want to see him. I just can't," I whisper to Tracy in desperation. I'm not ready. I grab the bottle of wine, pour another glass, and down that one too.

"Whoa, Nelly … no need to drink the entire bottle," Tracy whispers back. "Calm down. We'll figure this out."

Because the two men are seated in a room right by the front entrance, they have a good view of everyone coming and going. It's not likely that we can leave without Raine or Bret seeing us walk out the door.

"Damn! Where's the bathroom?" I whisper. I don't know why we are whispering. There is no way they can hear us from across the room, but I can't help it. Plus, I can't seem to catch my breath and a whisper is all I can get out.

"Let's go," Tracy says.

Tracy instantly stands and crouches down, as if this will help hide her, but few in the room will miss us as we scurry toward the refuge of the bathroom. I grab my purse and follow her, and once in the confines of the women's room, I dig inside my bag for a mirror and my lip gloss. Tracy watches me, her eyes still wide as I struggle with the contents of my bag.

"What do we do? If we try to leave, he'll see me!" My eyes go from Tracy to a long mirror as I nervously straighten my dress and fuss with my hair.

"Maybe this is a good thing? You can get this reunion out of the way. Then you won't have to worry about running into him and can concentrate on winning the show."

"Right now, all I want to do is get out of Vegas! Look." I hold out my hands and they are visibly shaking. "I can't see him right now. I'm a wreck and he's going to notice I'm a wreck."

I stagger to a bathroom lounge chair and fling myself onto the seat, my head dropping to my hands.

"I think I can get us out of here, hang on," she says, slipping out the door, leaving me alone in my despair. A few minutes pass and Tracy returns with our server, who gives me a sympathetic smile.

"It's all taken care of," Tracy says, kneeling in front of me and grabbing my hands to reassure me. I'm still frozen on the lounger. "Olivia here, our fantastic server, is going to lead us down the stairs and out the back of the restaurant. The bill's paid and it's all handled."

I look up at them, my slouching shoulders rising with this hopeful news, "Really? Oh my gosh ... you're an angel. Yes, let's get out of here."

I rise, grabbing my purse, and with as much courage as I can muster, I grab

Tracy's hand and take a deep breath as we make our way out the bathroom door. We both crouch down, as if we can hide behind Olivia, as she leads us down the stairs toward the back kitchen door. I glance back once at the small room where I know Raine is having dinner, and my feet tangle up with Tracy's. We almost tumble. She glances back at me scowling. A fall would create a scene. I'm shaken, but we make it to the kitchen and head toward the saving grace of those beautiful steel double doors that will lead me to safety.

I turn and give Olivia a grateful smile as we exit the restaurant. We're in some sort of back hallway. It's a bit dark, and restaurant gear crowds the aisle as I follow along behind Tracy, never losing her grip.

"Do you know where we're going?" I ask, jokingly.

"Not a clue," she says. "We're in a hotel … there has to be an exit around here somewhere."

And just like that, an exit sign appears to our right, we push open the big heavy door, and then we're out into the night air. Instantly, I can breathe again. We made it. That was close.

After taking a few steps down the street, Tracy finally asks, "Okay … so what is the big deal? I know you said you're not ready, but you're stronger than that, Jules. Why didn't we just go into that room and get it over with?"

"What would I tell him? I'd have to lie about why I'm here. Plus, I don't have anything to show him yet." When I say it aloud, I realize it's the first time I've admitted this to myself. I want him to realize what he gave up, and right now, that's nothing. He always seemed to want someone younger and more successful. I was never enough. I continue, "I need to be on the show with some success so I can stand tall around him."

Tracy nods at me, but she gives me that look I've seen before. It's the "I'm a big dope" look. And she may be right, but I've seen and experienced Raine's rejection before.

"He did look good though, didn't he," I say with a sigh. I can't help it. Raine did look good and, in my eyes, as handsome as ever. Tracy looks at me and rolls her eyes as we walk down the street and away from that man. Then it hits me hard; he's here in Vegas. Damn that man.

Chapter Eight – Julia

It's finally our first show day. I spent the last day and a half killing time with Tracy. I did get a much-needed massage, and went all out for a pedicure, manicure, the whole nine yards, but it didn't really help. I don't want to check my blood pressure. It's through the roof.

My car pulls up to the backstage door of the arena, which has a large canopy covering the entrance. Obviously, this is to keep the paparazzi from seeing who is entering or leaving this first rehearsal. The night before, Tracy and I ordered room service and watched the ACMs. As a guest of the reality show, I'm now under strict rules to maintain a low profile, so we couldn't really leave the room that much. The show's producers want secrecy to create as much buzz as possible.

During the ACMs, I caught a glimpse of Raine as the cameras briefly cut to him, and my stomach tightened. Bret was up for a fan-voted award but so was Catrina Smith, the biggest-selling country female artist in the last decade, so Bret really didn't stand a chance. Bret sang a new song he had co-written with Raine. Although I shouldn't be, I'm proud of Raine. I know how hard he works.

As I walk inside the backstage door, one of the show's assistants greets me. "Julia! I recognize you from your audition tape. Welcome!"

Wow. The staff is much friendlier than before. It's a welcomed but noticeable change from last time when I was a faceless auditioner.

I reply, "Hey, thanks! Glad to be here. What's the schedule for today?"

"You're rehearsing right after the last male contestant rehearses. You'll be the first female contestant during the show, number eleven. We're just finishing up with the contestant before you, and then the band will be ready for your song. We need you to wait in the green room. We're trying to keep everyone's identity a secret."

I nod along to everything he's saying, taking special note that I'm the first female contestant during the show. That's a plus, but I'll still have to wait a long time to perform. I take a deep breath, trying to calm my already frazzled nerves.

When it's time for me to rehearse, I'm standing on the side of the stage, and I glance out at the empty arena. As usual, my heart is pounding, and I can't seem to catch my breath. But one thought keeps running through my mind. How lucky can I be to have a chance like this, especially at my age?

When it's time, I take a moment to gather myself together. I carry my guitar and I walk to the center of the stage, turning to greet the band. I recognize a few faces from the audition, and they smile in return.

For this first show, we're required to play our audition song. As I start the first few notes, my voice shakes a little, but by the second sentence, I'm finding my groove and the band follows along effortlessly. Again, I'm in my element and the music flows out of me with ease. As I sing, thoughts of Raine and how he broke my heart fill my mind. I feel each word I'm singing and am more alive than ever. I have a reality show to win.

Later that night as I get ready for the show, my cell phone buzzes with texts from my sister Jody, wishing me well. This doesn't help my nerves. My whole body is shaking.

Although my family doesn't know I'm performing, Jody will call everyone before the show starts, telling them to watch. That's it. That's all she can say. I cannot blow it and make a complete fool of myself in front of millions of viewers, not to mention my family. Now there's a tough audience, I think with a smile. My family would never let me live it down.

A stylist is helping me get ready as I try to focus on controlling the butterflies and gurgling stomach. I pull my notebook out and rewrite the song lyrics over and over. Even though I know the song like the back of my hand, it helps me focus. This is one of the biggest nights of my life, and preparation will help me take a little control of the situation.

Before I head down to my waiting car, I look long and hard at my reflection in the mirror. Then I bow my head and say a silent prayer. *I pray to not only do well, but I thank God for giving me this chance to live my dream.*

My car makes its way to the backstage door area. I have no idea who I'm up against. My phone is buzzing with texts from Jody and Tracy wishing me well. I feel so blessed to have two amazing people in my corner.

I pull up to the backstage area at the arena and a mass of people, some with cameras, crowd the stage entrance, trying to get a glimpse of anyone. The dark tinted windows of my car and the canopy hide me from the onlookers' view. With the help of security, it looks like no one will get a picture of any contestant.

Once I get out of the car, I'm quickly escorted to a green room. As I walk into the room, I'm greeted by show staffers, and I finally get to see my competition. A couple of younger girls are sitting in front of mirrors, touching up their makeup.

I take a seat by the two singers, and we all exchange pleasantries. They both look as nervous as I am. I find out their names. Tiffany, a young blonde, is in the first chair, and Monica, a young African American girl, is next to her. Although everyone tries to act like this isn't the biggest night of our lives, I've been around the block long enough to know the girls are freaked out. I admit, I'm freaked out too, and this isn't my first rodeo.

I open my guitar case and start to tune my guitar right before a stagehand takes it to give to a guitar tech. I give him a huge smile. I've always wanted a guitar tech. I turn toward the mirrors in front of me and take a mental picture of this moment. I open my bags, pulling out my makeup case so I can touch up my face and hair.

The room buzzes with excitement as more contestants arrive and production assistants run in and out of the room. I try to focus on my makeup, but my hands aren't helping me. I can't keep them still. I take a deep breath, close my eyes, and visualize performing for the audience. In just a short while, I'll have the chance to make my vision a reality.

As more and more contestants enter the room, we all meet, slowly getting to know one another. Aubrey, a contestant sitting next to me, is closer to my age. We instantly form a bond. She has shorter blonde hair, breathtaking blue eyes, and to say she's beautiful is an understatement. Aubrey's gorgeous, like Marilyn Monroe, and there is something soft and fragile to her appearance.

Aubrey speaks first, "I hear you're from Nebraska. Small world. I grew up in Oklahoma, but now I live in New York. I spent many years on Broadway."

I lean over and shake her hand. "Good to meet you and glad to see someone else of legal age," I say with a laugh. "That's not a slight by the way, but I'm glad to see someone closer to my age."

"No offense taken. I was about to say the same thing. Are you a country performer?"

"I've done about everything, but now I sing more mainstream country with a bit of a pop influence. And you? What do you do now?"

"Rock. I'm a rocker," she says, smiling, her bright blue eyes glowing along with her smile. She seems genuine and warm.

"Cool. Well, good luck. I really mean that. It's hard enough in this business especially over the age of twenty-four."

"Same to you," Aubrey says sincerely.

I believe I may have found a friend in this weird, competitive world.

Earlier, the show's producers explained that they'll introduce the judges, and then after all the performances, they'll open it up to voting. Every contestant will get a score from the judges and once we are off the air, the world can vote, but only by computer or smart phone. Every vote must be digital—no phone calls. They are also limiting votes to one per email address and one per text.

A stagehand yells into the room, "Five minutes!"

Instantly, the room buzzes even louder. As has happened before, I think I might really get sick. I haven't been this nervous in years, if ever, but I must pull myself together. The show has set up a large flat screen in the room, and we all start to gather around it. When the show starts, they'll reveal the judges. Although my nervousness has now traveled to every muscle in my body and my legs are like mush, this is an exhilarating moment.

Chapter Nine – Raine

Show day arrives and from the moment I wake up, I'm busy with texts and calls for my real job back in Nashville, putting the finishing touches on my wardrobe for this first show, and squeezing in a celebratory lunch with Bret. Although he didn't win an ACM, we had a good, productive year.

"So, what's the plan for you these next few days?" Bret says with a smug, all-knowing grin on his face. He crosses his muscular arms and looks at me expectantly, his brown eyes dancing.

"I have no idea what you are talking about," I say, with as much innocence as I can muster. Although Bret knows about the show, I haven't given him any details.

"Right. The first show is tonight. The producers called and asked me to be in the audience."

"Oh, well, then I guess you know more than I do," I say with a shrug. "Sometimes I wonder what the hell I'm doing out here. I'm not a celebrity."

"But you are about to be, and then you'll see what it's like in the fishbowl."

"You make it sound terrible."

"It's not terrible. Just different. You'll see."

And for the first time, the nerves kick in. I hope I don't make a fool of myself on national television. What have I really gotten myself into? I'm realizing I'm more nervous than I thought I would be. I'm about to be introduced to millions of people. My face flushes at the thought, and I start to sweat. I pull the napkin from my lap and dab my brow.

Bret continues talking, but I'm having a hard time paying attention to his words. Not only am I now freaked out about the show, but I'm also constantly scanning the faces in the restaurant, looking for Julia. Don't ask me why.

Bret brings me back to reality. "Hey … are you listening? I just told you I took a call from one of the biggest country icons in our industry, who wants to write with us, and you said, "uh-huh." You haven't heard one word."

"Sorry, man," I say, before continuing, "I can't shake the feeling that Julia is here. It's like that old wives' tale that your nose itches when someone is thinking about you, and mine is itching like crazy."

Bret brings up the elephant in the room, "I could send her a text, and just mention the show?"

"I thought about that, but she's too smart. I haven't talked to her in years. She'd know something was up. After the show airs, maybe you can send her a text and ask if she watched. It'd be good to know." Then we continue on with our lunch, with me trying to focus.

##

Back at the hotel, my stylist is putting the finishing touches on my hair. I'm dressed in a black suit with a silver tie. Nerves, in the form of sweat, are now emanating from every pore, and whether I like it or not, I'm headed into this new chapter.

After tonight, the truth about my part in the show will be revealed. I hope that somehow, someway, Julia is watching.

I take another look in the mirror, and then take a big breath, slowly exhaling, hoping it will calm my nerves. This is one of the biggest, most life-changing nights of my life.

##

My driver pulls up to the backstage area, and when I arrive, I'm ushered through a door for the judges and dignitaries. The judges are being kept away from the performers, but when I walk into the green room, I find out who my two fellow judges are: Brandi Singleton, one of the most amazing, hottest female pop recording artists of all-time, and Davis Morrison, lead singer of the rock band Crush. I'm the only judge from the country arena, and as the show's token producer, I think I'll offer more of an outsider's marketing and stylistic viewpoint, which is much different from that of performers Brandi and Davis.

We're introduced, and then I'm led to a makeup chair. In only one hour the show will start, and my life will change.

I check my phone and notice a text from Bret. "I know you're nervous. Don't do something stupid like faint."

I text back, 'Thanks for the advice. You're all heart, dick head.'

But I am nervous, and I can't seem to stop sweating. I look in the mirror and let out a heavy sigh. I've performed for thousands of people, and worked with all kinds of celebrities, but am I up for this? The exposure will be great for my career, but I just hope like hell that Julia will be watching, because that's the real reason that I'm putting myself through this.

I hold out one of my hands and it's shaking. Damn it. Millions of people will be watching. I cannot embarrass myself and I've got to pull my shit together.

A makeup artist starts applying show makeup to my face, turning my slightly olive complexion into an unnatural bronze. When she walks away, I glance at myself in the mirror. I have a fake, overdone face, and I can't help but laugh at my reflection.

Chapter Ten – Julia

"Ladies and gentlemen, we are counting down in five, four, three, two, one," and then the stage manager points to the host of *Next Real Star*. Even the host is a secret, and we're all surprised when Katy Reynolds, former member of one of the hottest female pop trios, faces the camera and greets the audience. Katy is wearing a short, fuchsia dress and matching platform boots, which looks amazing with her mocha skin and jet-black hair. She's absolutely stunning.

"Good evening and thank you for tuning in to *Next Real Star*, where you and our surprise celebrity judges will choose the next original music star who'll take the world by storm," Katy says, directly into the camera. Katy continues and takes the show to its first break.

I nervously primp, along with everyone else, through the first round of commercials. When they go back on air, we again crowd around the television. I'm watching with trepidation as they announce the judges. I know they'll pick great people, but I hope the judges will be open-minded to an older performer. When they announce Brandi, several others in the room shriek and jump up and down. I smile to myself. Brandi's in her thirties now and will make a fair and knowledgeable judge.

As they start to announce the second judge, a cold shiver goes down my spine. When they say the name Bret Savage, I instantly know who they are talking about before they say Raine's name. Oh no …

"Are you okay?" Aubrey asks, standing next to me. My hand reflexively went to my throat, and I'm sure I look as pale as a ghost.

I pause slightly, trying to regain my composure as I stammer, "Um … yeah

… just a little nervous, I guess."

"Don't worry about it, you'll be great. At least you are the first female contestant, you can get it over with."

Aubrey lightly touches my arm and continues to watch the screen as the final judge is revealed, but I can't breathe. I'm shell-shocked and unable to move. How am I ever going to sing my song? Raine fucking Wagner is a judge? He'll be sitting just a few feet from me as I sing about him. He hasn't heard me sing for years and has never really heard me play guitar. It would be one thing if he were watching from hundreds of miles away, but not in the same room, just steps away from me in front of a screaming audience and television cameras.

I can't feel my hands and for a moment, I think I will actually faint. I don't hear Katy announce rock icon Davis Morrison as the third judge. I don't care. I'm in real trouble and pretty sure I'm going to lose my dinner in the green room.

I turn toward the television as the first male contestant walks onstage to sing. Ten men will perform, and then it will be my turn. It's a two-hour show, and I'm going to have to wait a full hour before I get to perform. One hour to try and keep my stomach in check and my scattered brain focused on what I'm here to do. I sigh heavily as I sit staring at my reflection in the makeup mirror, and a look of hopelessness stares back at me. I have no idea how I'm going to make it through this. I'm desperate, fearing I won't be able to get my legs to physically walk out on that stage. I put my head down and make a silent plea, *please God … let me get through this song without losing it on national television. Please help me sing in front of Raine and the entire world.*

For the next hour, the male contestants are all a blur. I don't hear a word they sing as I sit writing and rewriting my lyrics in my notebook. For some reason, all my lyrics have escaped my mind, so I'm writing and rewriting my words to help me remember them. Finally, as male artist number nine walks out, a stagehand comes up and taps me on the shoulder.

"Ms. Tate … you're about to go on."

I smile up at him weakly and nod as he leads me out the door. I glance back into the room as my new friend Aubrey gives me a thumbs-up, but the rest of the women are oblivious, caught up in their own preparation. I give a half-hearted smile back at Aubrey, and then walk out like Marie Antoinette headed toward the guillotine.

##

I'm now standing on the side of the stage, and it seems horrible to be me right now. I wish I were any place else at this very moment. As Katy introduces me as the first female contestant, my legs shake uncontrollably, and I try to catch my breath. I have to figure out how to erase the screaming audience, television cameras, and most especially, Raine, who will be sitting just feet in front of me, from my mind. It's taking everything to keep the bile down.

Katy finishes her introduction, and it's the moment of truth. I catch the eyes of the band's guitar player, who gives me an encouraging smile. I smile back and stand up a little straighter, determined to walk on the stage with confidence. This is my moment. I have earned this chance and I know Tracy, my sister, and everyone back home will have my back. I'm trying desperately to erase Raine from my mind. I have no idea what he's going to think about this, but I'm about to walk on the stage and find out.

Chapter Eleven – Raine

I'm on the side of the stage, pacing and having second thoughts. Reality is hitting me hard and I don't know if I'll make it onto the stage. Seriously? What am I doing here and what was I thinking? The world knows who Brandi and Davis are, but how did I get into this group? This is going to be a disaster. Sweat pours down my brow and my dark hair has so many products in it, I don't think it will ever move again. Brandi, Davis, and I each wait for our introductions. They'll start with Brandi, then me, and finally Davis.

I glance down as my phone buzzes with another message from Bret, 'Don't lock your knees and breathe or as I said, you'll faint.'

I reply, 'Leave me alone, dip shit. I've got this.' Bret is driving me nuts.

Katy comes back on the air. "Now it's time to reveal our celebrity judges. Everyone knows this first judge. An amazing performer, dancer, and songwriter ... please welcome ... Brandi Singleton!"

The crowd erupts as Brandi makes her way across the stage. After she sits in the middle judge chair in front of the stage, she turns and waves to the screaming audience.

"Next, we are going to introduce you to one of the most successful country music producers in Nashville. The brutally straightforward, acclaimed songwriter and award-winning producer of Bret Savage ... Raine Wagner!"

The crowd erupts again as I make my way across the stage. The audience isn't as loud as they were with Brandi, but they show me respect. I wave to the throngs of screaming live audience viewers and go down the steps to sit at Brandi's left-hand side.

##

At the first commercial break, stylists run out to where I'm sitting with the other judges and touch up my face and dab my brow, which more than glistens. I look back at the audience, and several young girls scream. How will I get used to this? I glance at my phone, and it's buzzing non-stop as people across the country are finding out I'm one of the celebrity judges.

Later, as each male contestant performs, we all respond to them verbally and then I write out a score up to one hundred points and hand this to a waiting production assistant. The world will help decide, but our scores will weigh heavily on who stays or leaves the show.

They take another commercial break after the last male performer, and I let out an enormous sigh. Halfway done and I've never felt this much pressure. I think about Bret, realizing a star performer doesn't have it easy.

Katy Reynolds walks back out on stage, ready to announce the first female contestant. Ten more contestants to go and we'll finally be done for the night. Then I'll have to answer to my friends and family across the country. Even though the night is filled with pressure, and I've never been so stressed, it seems great to be me right now.

As the break ends, Katy begins to explain the first female contestant's story, and it strikes me as oddly familiar. This performer had many opportunities for a successful career in her past, but never got a break. She now lives in Nebraska and is taking another chance. I freeze in my seat and literally my breath catches in my throat. Could it be? Is it Julia?

My question is soon answered as they announce her name and Julia boldly walks across the stage. I gasp. She smiles toward the camera in front of her and briefly catches my eye. The one woman I have been thinking about nonstop and have wanted another chance with is about to sing for me and millions of television viewers. If I thought I was sweating before, that was nothing. Anxiety spreads through me like fire. I glance back at the audience as they watch Julia walk across the stage toward the microphone. I'm suddenly filled with fear. I only want her to do well.

I cross my arms tightly across my chest and try to breathe. I'm struck by Julia's confidence and the gorgeous long red dress she is wearing. She's breathtaking. As she turns toward the audience and starts to play, I lose the crowd around me and become enthralled by the performer standing on stage at that very moment.

Chapter Twelve – Julia

I somehow gather strength I never knew I possessed. The band clicks right into groove with me as I play my opening chords, and then I turn toward the microphone, and give the audience a slight smile as I start to sing.

Just like at my audition, I overcome my nerves and I take control, commanding the stage. I glance out at the crowd, trying not to look at Raine, but I can see him sitting with his arms crossed, watching me intently. As I sing my lyrics, I think about him.

The screaming crowd is now quiet, mesmerized by my words of hope, healing, and strength. This isn't a song written about teenage angst, but true words from someone who has lived a life of regret and losing the love of your life. In this moment, Raine will probably know it is about him. It's too personal, but I don't care. As I hit the last note and the last chord of my guitar rings out, the crowd erupts. It's so loud I can't hear Katy or anyone else talk for a few moments.

I put my guitar down and walk to where Katy is standing. It's time for the judges to say a few words, and they start with Brandi. "Girl ... my, oh my! You set the bar high with that song," she says with excitement before continuing, "Amazing lyrics and good chord progressions. An incredible start to our women's portion of the show. Well done!"

Davis chimes in, "I completely agree with Brandi. Good chord progressions on your song, and it was slightly different than your typical country song. You have an amazing tone, and your voice has a pureness to it. It really was a beautiful performance."

I nod and smile toward Davis. Next is Raine. The air is thick, and time seems to stop. My stomach turns as he pauses before he speaks.

"Right ... right. I thought it was a good song, and your voice complemented the melody. A nice job," Raine says dryly. He doesn't smile and he looks uncomfortable, almost bored. Unlike the other two judges, his words lack any enthusiasm, and he barely looks at me.

Wow. Disappointment hits me, settling in the pit of my stomach. That's it? Raine's comments, in comparison to the other two judges, are noticeably less complimentary. The crowd boos, obviously not agreeing with Raine's assessment. He's known for being incredibly straightforward, and he didn't disappoint.

"Easy, everyone, easy," Katy says. "That's one judge's opinion."

The camera flashes to Raine, who's frowning. I smile at Katy and toward the camera, determined not to show my disappointment at his words. As Katy finishes and I walk offstage, the reality of what I've done hits me like a ton of bricks, and I stumble slightly just as I make it out of view. Luckily, an onlooker is standing close by and catches my arm. I glance up and recognize my temporary savior, a songwriter I went out with a few times in Nashville. Trent Austin is smiling openly at me; his gorgeous grin and deep dimples make him hard to miss.

"Girl ... why didn't you ever tell me you could sing and write like that? I would have married you in an instant," Trent says, smiling broadly at me.

I'm caught off guard by his statement but manage to laugh, more from nerves than anything. "Hey, Trent ... thanks. Just my little secret," I say, giving him a slight smile back. I'm still a bit overcome and clearly haven't regained my composure.

"Well, good luck to you, darlin'," he says, his strong southern drawl coming through. "That was amazing. I think you'll move on."

Trent smiles at me broadly, still holding my hand, and I must admit, my knees are a little weak. It probably has more to do with singing for Raine and millions of viewers, but Trent, who is slightly taller than me, has jet-blue eyes and a chiseled jawline. He's an incredibly good-looking man, so that might play a part.

At least one man appreciates my talent, I think as I walk away toward the dressing room, but my heart is heavy. Sure, this is my big chance for success, but wow, now I have to win Raine's approval too? And it's not just the show, I'd want his approval even if he wasn't a judge. I'm shaking my head in disbelief as I open the door to my temporary sanctuary. I cannot believe this. Raine Wagner will help decide the fate of my musical career. It makes my head spin.

As I walk into the dressing room, several of my competitors smile and cheer. At least it seems like a supportive group. I smile back appreciatively and find Aubrey, who sincerely looks happy for me.

"You were great," Aubrey says with a big smile. "I hope I can keep my you-know-what together like that."

I smile back. "I'm sure you will. Knock 'em dead," I say as Aubrey heads to the stage.

I find my chair and collapse, the weight of what I've just done washing over me, and although I know I did very well, Raine's comments hit me hard. Of any person on this earth, I want him to be blown away, but his comments were so blasé, like he wasn't really listening. Brandi and Davis liked it, so that has to mean something, but Raine, wow, he acted like he was watching paint dry.

My phone is blowing up with texts. The first person I go to is Tracy, who was in the audience.

'WTF!!!' is all Tracy texts.

I respond back, 'I know. WTF. I'll see you back at the hotel and we'll talk about it.'

Then it hits me. What if the producers find out I used to date Raine? If I thought my heart was heavy before, it now feels like a ton of bricks. My chance may be over before it even started. If anyone finds out about me and Raine it won't look right, even if it is an old relationship. This is doomed. This could shatter all my hopes and dreams.

Chapter Thirteen – Julia

Backstage after the show, I've changed into a short gold and white dress with tall platforms for the after-party with all the other contestants, judges, and show staff. This is the first time we'll all meet, which means Raine and I will be in the same room. What the hell am I going to do? I look down at my hands and notice they haven't quit shaking. I think I'm more terrified of being face to face with Raine than I was singing for millions.

I gather my strength and walk in, noticing I'm the oldest person in the room, but with my platforms, I stand tall. I straighten my back as much as possible, hoping that will lift my confidence. I casually walk around the room, and a few of the show's producers congratulate me on my performance. I go around and thank each band member, and out of the corner of my eye, I catch Raine enter the room. His eyes instantly meet mine. He nods slightly, no emotion showing on his face as he turns to greet one of the male contestants.

At that same moment, Trent appears in front of me. "You look even more amazing than you did on stage," he says, with an obvious appreciative scan up and down my body. "Dang, girl!"

"Thanks, Trent," I say sweetly, leaning in to give him a distant hug. Out of the corner of my eye, I can see Raine watching. Trent is standing close to me as a photographer walks up and takes a picture of the two of us. Trent leans in and puts his arm around my shoulder. I automatically smile toward the camera. One of the producers notices us, and remarks how good we look together. Trent smiles down at me, and I can't help but glance toward Raine, who is watching the scene, scowling fiercely.

Raine and I each slowly make the rounds, and I watch him from the corner of my eye as he greets other contestants and freely talks with the band, like he doesn't have a care in the world. It's obvious we're trying to keep our distance but it's inevitable that we are going to have to speak as we both walk around the room. The space between us gets smaller and smaller, and my breath becomes even more shallow. As we get closer to one another, my eyes start darting back and forth toward him until, at last, we are standing face to face.

Raine is well over six feet tall. Even in my platforms, he towers over me. This is the first chance I've been able to really look at him, and God, he has hardly changed. He still cuts an imposing figure, tall, dark, with striking facial features. His green eyes, which at times can be so soft they'll make you melt, are framed with long, dark lashes, but his face is very masculine with sharp angles, and a very strong jawline. It's hard for me not to stare at him. His face hasn't changed much, there are just a few more lines and a light touch of gray around his temples, which makes him even more handsome. Coupled with how amazing he smells, I'm struggling to breathe. Being this close to him is so distracting that I'll have to focus on every word and move I'm making.

Raine leans slightly toward me, extending his hand as he says, "Julia, good to meet you, enjoyed your performance."

I give him a "that's all you have to say?" look as I extend my hand back and lean up slightly toward his face to say quietly, a grin pasted on my face, "What in the Sam Hill? Do you have any idea how shocked I was when you walked out?"

Raine smiles back at me and says quietly, "Now is not the time or place. I was equally as surprised. We have to keep our cool."

"No shit," I say back, my pasted-on smile still glued in place, but my eyes are fierce as they bore into his.

Raine frowns at me before quietly responding, "We'll have to talk about this. No one can find out about us."

"Agreed," I say under slightly clenched teeth, still with my pasted-on smile, as if I'm enjoying every word passing between us.

Raine's eyes soften. "Julia, you did a great job tonight, I want you to know that. I'm really proud of you."

My heart skips, and for a moment my eyes soften as they look into his eyes. I was not prepared for him to say anything nice. That's not the Raine I know.

Raine quickly continues, "I'll send you a text and we'll talk about this."

With that, he turns and walks away to the next person in the room. I'm shaken for a moment as I watch him walk away. Not only because the man I vowed to hate for all eternity was standing just a few feet from me, but because of every word he just said, how he looked, smelled, and most importantly, the turmoil of knowing the fate of my career is in his hands.

Aubrey comes up to me as Raine walks away, bringing me out of my daze, "What do you think of Raine?" she asks, stepping to my side. "He's from Nashville, right?"

"Yeah ... he is," I stammer. "But so is Trent," I say, nodding in his direction. I want to divert Aubrey away from Raine as quickly as possible.

"He's a cute one ... do you know Trent well?"

"Fairly well. He's a good guy but a smooth talker," I say with a knowing grin, before adding, "I met Trent before he became famous. He's still the same nice guy he was years ago."

Aubrey nods and then gestures around the room. "I'm gonna get out of here and clear my head for a while. Wanna find a bar and get a drink?"

"Maybe next time. We've got a big promo day tomorrow. I'm the 'old lady' and I'd better get back to the hotel and get some rest."

"Okay, girl. Good job today."

"You, too. Really good. I'll see you tomorrow," I say, leaning in to give Aubrey a quick hug.

I turn and head back to the green room to gather up all my stuff, hopeful I can make a ghost-like exit from the arena. It's been a tough, but good night, and I'm more than exhausted. I can feel Raine's eyes on me as I make my way out the door.

A waiting stagehand calls out to get security so they can get me to my car. As my car reaches the hotel's main stairs, there are several fans camped out in front of the hotel. Camera's flash and girls scream as I step out. This is the first time I've ever been asked for an autograph, and I smile as the fans press close. I sign as many items as possible and lean in for a few selfies. Finally, I squeeze my way through the crowd and up to my room.

As I close and lock my door, I let out a huge, heavy sigh and drop my bags on the floor. Tracy, who has already returned, walks out of the bathroom, and says, "Raine Wagner? What in the world?"

I roll my eyes at her, walk over to my king size bed, and fling myself on top of the covers, exhausted, exhilarated, and overwhelmed. My conflicted head is aching. Finally, I say, "Having a prior relationship with a judge will not look good, Trace, not to anyone. But how do I give this up? This is everything I've ever wanted."

Tracy looks at me, shakes her head, and shrugs. "I don't even know what to say to you right now."

I continue, "I do know one thing, I'm going to have to see Raine, and a lot of him. Oh God, this is terrible." But deep down I know that standing just a few feet from him tonight, if only for a few minutes, got my heart aching to see him again. All I can think about is wanting to feel those strong arms around me. Damn. That. Man.

Chapter Fourteen – Raine

As my driver heads back to the hotel, I can't stop thinking about Julia and her performance. I judged the competition fairly, but Julia's performance was outstanding. She's clearly a standout among the other female competitors. I gave her a good, but fair score. Julia's lyrics hit me hard. Her song was about losing love and recovering, and in my heart, with all that I put her through, I wonder if it was about me.

Bret sends me a text, 'What the … are you kidding me?? She was AMAZING.'

Of course Bret is talking about Julia. I don't respond. I can't think clearly right now.

Since we are both a part of the show, as I said to Julia, no one can find out about us. This is my shot for national recognition, and I don't want to ruin her chances, but *damn it*! Standing that close to her at the after-party, and not even being able to give her a simple hug, was excruciating. God, she looked and smelled amazing, just as I imagined. I physically ached from being that close to her, and I couldn't help telling her how proud I was that she'd taken this step. Truly a calling she'd almost missed. Although it's a terrible idea, all I want right now is to talk to her and see her again, tonight if possible.

As soon as I make it back to my room, I send Julia a text, asking to see her. I've been waiting for a reply.

Several minutes pass and Julia finally sends me a text back, giving me her room number, which I realize is bold on her part. I text back that I'll see her in a few minutes. I need to get this television makeup off first.

I clean up, change, and quietly poke my head out my door, glancing around the hall. I don't see anyone, but I'm extra careful to make sure no one notices me head toward Julia's room. She's a couple floors below and I take the stairs to be safe.

Outside of her door, I pause, composing myself, and then softly knock. Julia answers, wearing pajamas, her hair piled on top of her head. I can tell she just got out of the shower. Even without makeup, she's gorgeous. She looks up at me quizzically as I enter the room, and once securely inside, it's all I can do not to take her in my arms. Instead, I shut the door behind me and lean against it, my arms behind my back. They're safer there and I'll be less inclined to gather her up in them.

I glance around looking for Tracy.

"Tracy went down to the casino," she says, clearly sensing I was wondering if we were alone.

I look directly into her eyes as I say, "Again, you have no idea how surprised I was to hear your name called."

Julia looks at me, her blue eyes have softened but she's standing with her arms crossed in front of her, clearly defensive. There's a fierceness in her tone. "You were surprised? I almost fainted when they announced you were a judge."

"I can't say much more than this, but again, I truly am so proud of you. I'm proud you went out on that stage, sang that song, and you looked so beautiful. It took my breath away."

Julia seems stunned and turns away before responding, "That's not what you insinuated to me on stage in front of millions of viewers." The fierceness in her eyes returns. "You actually seemed quite bored," she says defensively.

"Julia ... I know you, quite intimately. I had to choose my words carefully during the show. You know we have to be very careful about everything we do and say," I reply, dropping my arms to my side, but I'm still leaning against the door, away from her. I can't get any closer. Her freshly showered and lightly perfumed body is affecting me physically and it's best that I stay as far away from her as possible. "Obviously, since we're in this predicament,

47

we have to continue to act like we don't know each other." I've started to fidget now. It's the only thing I can do to distract myself from everything about her.

"Of course," she says, looking up at me. I can't read her eyes, but the stern look on her face, tight lips, and stance are a good indication of how she's feeling.

"Okay, well, I want you to have this chance and I want it too … but again, I'm so glad you took this step," I say without betraying my real thoughts about her amazing performance, and the fact that all I want to do is carry her over to her inviting bed, which already has the covers pulled down. I glance at the bed, and she follows my eyes.

"Well, then I guess that's all there is," she says, walking toward me and the door, a clear indication that I need to go.

I turn around, start to open the door, and then pause, my back to her. She is still a few feet away from me and I speak so quietly that I'm not sure she hears, "You did look beautiful tonight, love the red dress." Then I quickly open the door, glance down the hall, and, seeing no one there, I'm out into the hallway. I hear the door shut firmly behind me.

I take the stairs back to my room. The full effect of having her that close overwhelms me. Damn, she's right here and I can't have her. How am I going to do this and not completely blow everything? I wanted to win Julia back, and now all this show is going to do is push her away. I walk to the bathroom for a much-needed cold shower.

Chapter Fifteen – Julia

The next morning, it's all I can do to get out of bed. I tossed and turned all night, and my pillow is still damp from tears. After Raine left the room, I crumpled to the ground right by the door and had a good, soul-drenching cry. All the years and what that man put me through, coupled with the emotions from having him so close, the words he said, and the toll of the day, were too much. How could this happen? How one man can come in and out of my life, nearly destroying me, and now this same man and prior relationship could nuke my singing career. I had to let it all out, but now this morning, I feel like a freight train has run over my head. I'm stuffy and I'm sure my eyes are swollen. Great.

I pull myself out of bed and make my way to the bathroom to shower and fix my face. How am I going to get through this?

The shower seems to help, as well as the pot of coffee I order. Then I spend a good hour trying to answer every text message and voicemail I have from friends and family about the show. Tracy had to fly out early and she's already gone, so the room is quiet. Too quiet. It's just me and all my mixed-up thoughts about Raine and how this will impact the show. I wish Tracy could have stayed longer. I'm not sure how I'll get through this on my own.

I manage to pull myself together, get dressed, and take the elevator down to the main floor and again, a legion of screaming fans surrounds me. A security guard helps me get through the crowd, and as I make my way to my car, I grasp hands with as many people as possible and pose for a few pictures. I don't know how I'll get used to people calling my name. It's exciting, yet out-of-body at the same time.

When I arrive back at the arena, the show's producers gather all the contestants in a staging area. Video cameras surround us, along with a few photographers. Today, we'll shoot video for promo purposes, and then we'll head over to a recording studio to prepare a song for the next show.

We find out the judges are off doing live interviews with the media, and for this, I'm grateful. After last night, I don't need Raine in the same room. It's all I can do to concentrate on what I need to do without having him around to distract me. The connection between us is still there, that's obvious. We're like two magnets, and if he's in the same room, I'm drawn to him. I need to stay as focused as possible, but Raine is never far from my mind. Between photo takes, I make small talk with Aubrey.

"My friends and family are floored, how about yours?" Aubrey asks as she sips coffee.

"Yep, a real shocker. I've spent hours trying to explain myself," I say with a laugh.

"What's up for the next show?"

"Not sure. One of the producers told me we'd find out more later today."

We continue with a few more promos, and then it's off to the recording studio. I've spent many years in studios, and its old hat for me, but for a few of the contestants, it's the first time they've ever recorded anything like this. Along with Aubrey, we end up giving a few pointers.

Although it's a grueling day, it passes quickly and before I know it, we're finishing up a group dinner and one of the producers is making announcements, "As you all know, we're working hard to separate this show from the gluttony of other reality shows. So, we have a surprise for you all. We'll team each one of you up with a Grammy award–winning songwriter for your next song. Everyone will perform during the next show, and no contestant will be sent home. But based on results of the combined opening show and this next performance show, will let four people go during the first results show in L.A."

An audible groan erupts from the group. "I know … it sounds like a lot," the producer says before continuing. "We want to get down to the final sixteen, then we'll cut to eight, and then down to four contestants for the final show. The good news is, not every show will be an elimination show. We want the television audience to get to know the contestants, so we'll shoot footage of you back in your hometowns, with family, friends, everything. We want America and the world to fall in love with each one of you. It's your best bet at having a career when the show is finished."

A murmur fills the room, and I'm filled with dread. Close scrutiny of my personal life is bound to bring up my previous relationship with Raine. Although we dated off and on, a few people know about us, too many people. If the world finds out about my relationship with Raine, how would anyone believe I legitimately made it on the show? As I sit contemplating what I'm going to do, I'm the quietest person in the room filled with excited chatter.

Chapter Sixteen – Raine

I'm with Brandi and Davis and we're busy meeting with the media. It's been a tough day, alternating between live interviews and trying to manage my "real job" back in Nashville. I've got to work with Bret and pick out new songs for his next project and finalize studio details back in Nashville. Not to mention all the calls from shocked friends and family about my appearance on the show. Every minute of my day is jam-packed.

Overnight, I've become a household name and even trended on Twitter. That's a new one. Even with all the excitement of the day, my mind rarely drifts away from seeing Julia's face, not to mention wishing I could touch various parts of her body. It's hard for me to concentrate.

At one point, I turn to Davis and make small talk. "After this, we'll tape a few segments and then we're free for the day, right?"

"I think so," Davis responds. My publicist is handling most of the details and just tells me where to show up and when. I've heard they're going to partner the contestants with Grammy-winning songwriters."

"I didn't know that. A good move. If you want to be in this business, you should bring in something fresh."

Davis nods, and then we're all quickly escorted out to the front stage for some close-up shots with products from the show's main sponsor.

So, they'll partner Julia with a Grammy-award winning producer? Instantly I picture her with some man and my stomach turns. It'd better be a woman, I think as my jealous nature takes over. And although it's a terrible idea, I want to see her and find out who it is.

##

Later that night, as I'm on my way to meet my new publicist for dinner, I consider sending Julia a text to ask about her writing partner but I change my mind. I'll seem desperate, which I am, but somehow my rational brain takes over. We've got to stay apart.

I pull up to a trendy restaurant, and a throng of anxious fans are standing outside of the building holding signs and screaming. I have no idea how they found me, and as I get out of the car, the crowd erupts. I've never been one for the public eye, but this is part of my new responsibility and I give a wave to the fans. Bret's label arranged for this publicist knowing I needed some help to manage the chaos, and based on what I'm experiencing, they're right.

I walk into the restaurant with security leading the way, and people around me stop and stare. Now I know what Bret meant by a "fishbowl." As I make my way toward my table, I run my hand through my dark hair and my mind drifts to Julia, wondering if she's going through the same thing.

Chapter Seventeen – Julia

Following dinner, we're all transported as a group back to the hotel where, again, we're greeted by screaming fans outside of the lobby. Tomorrow, each of us will be assigned a Grammy-winning writing partner and will begin to immediately work on a new song. At last count, more than thirty-eight million votes had been counted, and they expect more.

I stagger, exhausted, to my room and once I'm inside, I collapse on my bed. Lying there, I glance at the closed door where Raine was standing just a few hours earlier, and my heart pounds. I shake my head trying to erase the vision of him leaning against the door I'm now staring at.

After a long, hot shower, I settle down with my phone. I see Raine's name and the text he sent last night, and my heart jumps. Conflicted emotions rage through my mind. I should erase his text, but I just stare at it. It's hard not to send him a message, but what would I say? "How's your day?" Nope, I came here to win this show and I'm going to prove to him that I can. I give Tracy a quick call instead.

Tracy picks up after one ring. "Julia Tate fan club."

"Girl, you're crazy … no, wait, *I* am for putting myself through this."

"You'll be fine … I still can't believe Raine's a judge though. I'm glad you got to talk to him."

I hesitate for just a moment and Tracy jumps to the wrong conclusion. "Did you sleep with him?"

"*NO!* No way. We agreed to stay away from each other, and that's what we're doing." But my anxious mind starts to spill all my fears as I rapidly blurt out, "But this has disaster written all over it. No one, and I mean no one, can find out we used to date. The producers would kick me off the show, it would hurt Raine's career, and my career would be ruined. I can't be anywhere near Raine. But the show is going to dig deeply into our lives ... I really don't know how this will remain a secret." Finally, I pause. "I want this chance. Trace, I deserve it."

Tracy responds calmly, "Just cross each bridge as you come to it. They may not find out. Although you dated Raine off and on for years, you weren't very public. Only a few close friends know about the two of you."

"Right, but how am I going to stay away from him? He's like a drug. Raine was in my room for less than two minutes, and I could barely keep my shit together."

"Just stay focused. Do you need me to come back and be your personal assistant to help you through this?"

Although Tracy is kidding, it sounds like a great idea, but neither of us have the money to fly her back out. "I'd love to have you come back out, but that's not realistic. I just need to stay away from Raine, although that's much easier said than done."

We talk a bit more about what will happen the next few days, but I keep many elements of the show a secret. Tracy offers to help drum up support, like a social media fan club, and I let her. I need as much help as I can get.

By the time I get off the phone with Tracy, it's late, and again, I think about texting Raine. But why would I? There's really no reason.

##

I only have two days to write and rehearse a new song before I perform again live. This morning, we're all taken to a sound studio where we each have our own rehearsal room. Now I'll find out who my writing partner is.

I'm more relaxed than I thought I would be at this point. Songwriting is my forte. I think I'm a better writer than a live performer, and I'm looking forward to this. After they give me a room number, I pick up my guitar and walk down a long hallway. As I open the door, I'm greeted by another surprise. Trent sits at the piano, plunking out a melody.

Trent gets up and walks toward me with a big smile on his face, his arms stretched open wide, as he says, "Well, I'll be … I had hoped they would assign you to me. Or is it me to you?"

I somewhat awkwardly greet his embrace. Although Trent's greeting is warm and inviting, I try not to hug him too tightly.

I reply back with excitement, knowing I'll be working with one of the best songwriters around, "I had no idea you were one of the writers! I'm so happy to get to work with you, Trent."

Trent has written huge songs for every major country icon you can think of and has dozens of number-one hits. I'm lucky to get him as my writing partner. I did go out with him a few times, so this may be a bit uncomfortable. Thank God we never slept together.

"I'm here to write a hit and help you win this show, although I don't think you need my help," he says appreciatively.

"Trent, you're amazing, and yes, I do need your help, believe me."

"Well, let's get to it. Any new ideas you want to start with?"

"I liked that melody you were playing," I say, nodding toward the piano. "Was that something we could use? It'd be good to write something on piano rather than guitar."

"Let's start with it and see what happens." Trent walks back to the piano and gestures for me to sit down next to him.

"Wait, I need to bring my crutch." I open my guitar case and grab my six-string. At the very least, it will help keep Trent at arm's length. He's way too cute and charming, and I don't need another distraction. He smiles as I pull up a chair beside him and we get down to business.

Chapter Eighteen – Raine

We finish recording promos and are finally free for the day. Tomorrow we'll have more interviews and promos to tape, but other than that, it's like having a very busy working vacation in Vegas. Distractions surround me, but I don't notice any of the pretty girls, and I don't want to gamble. I need to get out and get some fresh air. Bret has stayed in Vegas for the next show, and we're meeting at a golf course to let off some steam.

"I heard they're getting professional writers to work with them," Bret says, while sitting in his golf cart as I walk out, readying myself for my first drive.

"How do you know that? It's supposed to be a secret."

Bret smirks. "I have my sources. I also hear they are partnering Julia with Trent Austin." He pauses, obviously waiting for my reaction.

I glance at his smug face, and casually turn away pulling a golf ball from my pants pocket and placing it on the tee. "Really? He's a good writer," I say as I put my club down and practice my swing. Then I swing the golf club, striking the tiny ball, truly answering Bret's statement. I hit the ball farther than I've probably ever hit that fucking thing before. The truth is, I'm pissed. My mind races. They put her with a male writing partner, and not just any guy, Trent, fucking, Austin. *Damn it!*

Bret shakes his head in amusement. "What are the two of you going to do?" he asks.

"Stay away from each other," I say as I pick my tee up out of the ground, trying to act like it's any other day. I turn directly toward him. "We have to. I want her to have this chance and I don't want to screw up my career either."

"You know I won't say a word, but someone could bring up the fact the two of you dated. You cannot be seen with her."

"Exactly … Have you been discussing this with my publicist?" I say, giving him a sideways glance.

"Never. I told you. Your secret is safe with me. I want Julia to win, and I think she's got a good chance. Why didn't you ever tell me she could sing and write like that? I would have put her on one of my albums."

"I didn't know."

"You two would have amazingly talented babies," Bret jokes.

I look straight at Bret, and then look away without saying a word. In my heart, that's what I want, and the truth of it shocks me. But I can't have her, at least not yet. What Bret said has hit a nerve though. Why do I care so much about the show? Julia is right in front of me, here and now. I should make my feelings known, I love her and always have. But instead, I'm playing golf with my best friend and trying to have a good time, while the love of my life is just a few miles away. I finally turn back and nod at him as we walk toward our carts so I can continue murdering golf balls. But something in my gut is telling me to call Julia or reach out in some way, or I may blow it again. Trent Austin. For fuck's sake. I swing my golf club into the ground, and it sends dirt flying into the air. Bret gives me a sideways glance, puts his head back, and laughs.

Chapter Nineteen – Julia

After an exhausting, but productive day writing with Trent, I'm finally heading back to my hotel. My car is easing down the Vegas strip as I stare out the window at the crowds of people, amazed at how quickly my life has changed. Just a few days ago, I wasn't a well-known singer and performer, but now I'm on a nationally broadcast show watched by millions. The brilliance of reality television is that it gives people a chance they may never have had.

The driver takes me to the back of the hotel, and swarms of young fans are there. I truly don't know how I'll get used to all this attention. I step out of the car and again smile and wave. A young girl holds up a sign with my name on it, and I walk over and sign it. A security team has been waiting for contestants and they help get me inside. I want to stop at a hotel restaurant, but figure room service will be easier.

When I get to the hotel room door, I'm amazed at who greets me.

"I told you I'd be your personal assistant," Tracy says, casually lounging in a chair in the hall.

"Oh my God! I can't believe you're back. This is wild! I could really use your help to keep my head on straight, but how did you get here?" I say as I excitedly run over and give my best friend a hug, and then I help her with her bags.

Tracy drops her stuff on the floor in my room and she answers my question, "Raine. He probably doesn't want you to know, but he paid for my flight."

"Wow ... that's surprising," I reply, and I pause because years ago, Raine would never have done something like this for me. This realization shocks me more than anything.

Tracy gives me a serious look. "How are you coping with everything?"

"I'm good," I say casually, omitting my raging Raine emotions. "Had a challenging but productive day. I think I've got a decent shot at this thing."

"I think you have more than a decent shot."

"All that matters is what the judges think. Their scores count more than anything and I'm not sure I've won them over yet. Raine is the only true country connection."

"Well, I'm sure he's in your corner," Tracy says, as she grabs a bottle of water and flings herself down into a chair. "You're a shoe-in."

"Even though he personally told me I did well, you heard what he said during the show, didn't you? He basically told me I was average in front of millions of viewers. That didn't help. And if anyone finds out about us, game over. People will think Raine is biased toward me."

Tracy nods in agreement. "Okay, changing the subject," she says with a smile before continuing, "I know you can't tell me anything, but what happened today?"

"Right," I say with a laugh. "I'm not biting. How about we order room service?"

"All right … all right. I can take a hint."

It relaxes me more than I realize to have Tracy here, and at the very least, it will help keep me entertained. After dinner and hanging out a bit, Tracy heads down to one of the casinos. At least she can get out and have some fun. I'm strolling around picking up the room when my phone buzzes. It's Raine.

He writes, "I know we said we can't see each other in public, but how about a casual dinner in my room tomorrow night? Just so we can catch up. I'd really like to see you, Jules."

And there it is. My heart is pounding. I should wait a few minutes before responding, but nope, against my better judgment I send a message right back. "Hey Raine, well, not sure it's a great idea, but I could meet with you for a quick dinner." And I think to myself, and that's all it will be. Dinner.

He takes seconds to reply, "Perfect, I'll send you a message when I'm back at the hotel and we'll set it up. Will be good to see you."

"Sounds good," I reply.

I walk over and sit on the bed, staring at my phone, knowing in my gut it's not a good idea, but I just couldn't say no. Of course, part of me is desperate to see him and wants to hear what he has to say, but the other part is screaming, *"don't do it!"* I do know I can't wait for him to hear the song I wrote with Trent. I hope he'll be floored by it. Yes, I want the world to hear the song, but there's only one person whose opinion really matters, and I will do everything in my power to prove to Raine that I deserve to win this show.

Chapter Twenty – Julia

The next day starts at 4:30 a.m., and I realize there just isn't enough coffee in the world. Tracy will keep herself busy as I head out for the day. I've told Tracy about my upcoming dinner plans with Raine, and she didn't seem surprised. Tracy seemed more concerned about what I was going to wear than my secret dinner with the one man I've sworn to hate for eternity.

When I arrive in the arena, there's a flurry of activity. I have a makeup artist and hairstylist trying to make me look as good as they can this early, and it's brutal. The bags under my eyes tell of the night I had, again tossing and turning. They dress me in a long, purple gown, with a slit that runs up my entire leg to my upper thigh. They're mixing Hollywood glamour with country and pop, and I love it.

Aubrey sits at a table next to me, and they are making her look very glam rock. I've never seen so much black eyeliner. Aubrey would give the rock gods a run for their money on makeup.

"Here we go. How are you coping?" Aubrey asks above the fray.

"Great! My best friend flew in last night to help. It's good to have some support. You'll need to meet her. I think you two would get along famously."

"I'd like that. My mom came into town, and you're right, it does help to have someone here, to help you get fed at least. I haven't been able to go anywhere by myself."

"I know. It's crazy! A good crazy, but crazy all the same."

We finish getting fixed up and then they walk us all out on the stage. Although we'll perform our recorded group song live, we have to lip-sync the background vocals to tracks, which will play along during the show. I don't like lip-syncing. If you can't do it live, you shouldn't be doing it at all, but I go along with it.

When I walk backstage, I see Raine. He's sitting in a chair and a makeup artist is finishing up his face. A pang of jealousy hits me. She's young and his typical type. Raine sees me enter and gives me a quick but semi-hidden wink, and I can't help but give him a slight smile back. Then I'm instantly nervous, skittish, and clumsy as I almost walk right into someone. He always has that effect on me. I glance back at him and he's smirking at me. He noticed.

We take our places and spend four grueling hours getting ten good promo spots. We hit our marks over and over before they finally call it a wrap. Now I have to tape a spot with just the judges. I'm going to have to stand close to Raine, and when it's our time to record, the air between the two of us gives me goosebumps. I wonder if anyone notices how he gets to me. Raine tries to play it cool, but I can see slight beads of sweat along his upper brow. He's as nervous as I am. The three judges surround me for our take, and they put Raine right behind me. I can literally feel his eyes on my ass, and at one point, his hand ever so lightly touches my backside, and I unconsciously shiver. I give a quick glance back at him as they are fixing the lighting, and he gives me an innocent smile. Damn him. Then I realize I'm more than glowing. Sweat is starting to pour. A makeup artist runs over and dabs my face. I can only imagine Raine behind me, watching the entire scene. We can't finish this spot soon enough. When we are done, I scurry away as fast as possible to the safety of my group.

Aubrey is standing there and asks, "You okay? You seemed nervous up there and you don't ever seem nervous."

I give Aubrey a half-hearted smile and try to pass it off as nothing. "Oh, I get nervous, I'm just usually better at covering it."

Aubrey nods, but she gives me an odd look as I continue to tap my brow with a tissue. That man. That fucking man. Now he's impacting my work. Yes, we'll have our dinner and I'll put an end to this.

When we're finished with the promo spots, I feel a tap on my shoulder.

"Hey, darlin'," Trent drawls. "Are you ready for our close-up?"

I whirl around, surprised, and quickly give Trent a hug. I can't help it. I'm caught up in my personal Raine anxiety hell and can't control my actions at this point. Raine is still finishing up promos and catches the entire scene with Trent. He's noticeably scowling. Here's my chance to get him back. I continue to make small talk with Trent, overdoing my flirty smiles, and I throw in a few laughs until it's time to finally break for lunch. Raine and the other judges aren't allowed to join us and have to leave the room. I watch Raine skulk off, and an innocent smile crosses my lips as he glances back at me before walking out the door. Trent and the other pro writers are allowed to hang with us. Trent sits backstage with me during our break, but I'm having a hard time concentrating.

"You're hardly eating a thing. You okay?" Trent asks, pulling me back to reality.

"I'm fine, just not very hungry. I've been stuck in a hotel room for days. Believe me, I'm eating," I say, but my thoughts are on my upcoming dinner with Raine.

As we're eating, a photographer comes up and takes a quick photo of me sitting next to Trent. When the photographer walks away, Trent sighs and quietly comments, "I remember fame well, it never got easy. It's better now that I'm no longer an artist, but still, I remember it."

"Are you happy as a writer, Trent? Do you miss performing?"

"I do miss it sometimes. I always wanted to be a rock star," he says with a laugh, his deepening dimples making him even more handsome, and then he continues, "Life turned out just as it should have. I have a great life and I get to write for a living. But what about you, what do you really want from all of this?"

"To be a stay-at-home mom," I semi-joke, with a laugh. "Seriously, I love to write. I like the performance side, too, but my heart is with writing."

"I think if your heart is being a married mother, that can be arranged," Trent says as he puts his hand on top of mine, giving me a knowing grin.

"I'm sure it could," I say sarcastically, smiling back at him, but pulling my hand away at the same time. Trent can lay it on thick and you can easily get lost in his gorgeous brown eyes, but I remind myself I have to stay strong. I have a show to win.

Chapter Twenty-One – Julia

I've been a wreck from the moment my car dropped me off at the hotel as I wait for Raine's text. Tracy interrupts my freak-out.

"Okay, the most important question is, what are you going to wear?" Tracy's smirking, but she's serious.

This is my first real meeting with my tormentor, and I have to look great. I've already pulled a shorter black satin dress with a tuxedo-style top, cut just above the knees, from the closet. It's form fitting and nicely accentuates my curves and waist. It's a size two and I'm proud of that. Prior to the show, I'd been working hard to stay in shape and that's not easy for a woman over forty. I've kept my hair down and it reaches past my shoulder blades. Tracy helps me touch up my makeup because she's better at it. While we are in mid-redo, my phone buzzes, and I jump.

Raine's message is brief, 'Just arrived back in my room. Could you give me an hour?'

With trembling hands, I send my reply, 'An hour it is.'

That hour takes a year as I pace around the room. I know I've overdone it. I'm dressed to kill in my dress and four-inch heels, but it's one way I think I can stay in control. As I'm about to head to his room, Tracy leans in to hug me.

"Stay strong and don't sleep with him," she says, pulling back to look directly in my eyes.

"What am I, new?" I joke back, but I need those words. Raine can work magic, and I must be strong. Even though I'm still angry with him, my heart is betraying me with every beat.

##

I quietly take the stairs to his room, cautiously looking down every hallway, every step of the way. You never know who you could run into at the hotel, and I have to be careful. I knock and Raine answers wearing a short-sleeved black dress shirt, which grips his biceps, and black slacks. He smiles as he opens the door, towering over me. Raine steps aside to let me in, and I'm taken aback by the scene before me. The room is dimly lit with candles, and there are purple tulips in a vase on a table in the center of the room. Room service delivered covered dishes that are waiting for us.

After I enter and Raine closes the door, he turns and gives me a slight embrace. It's awkward but comforting in a way. I guess it's more of a habit than anything. Then Raine nervously fidgets with his shirt collar.

"It's good to see you," he says, standing a good five feet from me, but even at this distance, I can smell his cologne. It's musky and intoxicating.

I smile back timidly, "Good to see you." My voice has taken on an odd, high pitch, which often happens when I'm extremely nervous. I continue, gesturing to the noticeable ambiance. "Wow, quite the setup."

Raine looks a bit sheepish, which is not in his character. "Well, it's been a long time and I wanted it to be special." He pauses slightly. "Even if we are trapped in this room."

Now he's staring straight at me and smiling, his eyes dancing, peering into my soul as only he can. This is the Raine I know, confident and sure of himself.

"Well, it's beautiful," I reply as he gestures toward my waiting seat at the table.

I take a seat as Raine walks to the table, picks up my wine glass, and pours a glass of Chardonnay. I sit still, watching him. There is something about him that's different. There is a softness to Raine that wasn't there before. I can sense it and it puts me on edge.

After Raine pours our wine, he walks over, uncovers our dinner plates, and brings one over, placing it in front of me. A rib-eye, just the way I like it, along with fresh vegetables. He grabs a plate with the same for himself and sits back down, giving me a quick up-and-down look as he does.

"New shoes?" Raine asks teasingly as his eyes crinkle up.

"Of course. You know I have a problem."

"I know. How do you ever find closets big enough for all your shoes?" he asks with a grin.

Then Raine, never one to beat around the bush, looks at me and cuts right to the chase, "So, I hear you're writing with Trent." His voice fades at the end of the sentence, and I notice. He then proceeds to cut into his steak as if he doesn't have a care in the world.

For some reason, I think I have to answer this one carefully. "I am. He's a great writer. We've got a good song going."

"Right, but I know how that guy works," he says, stabbing into his rib-eye with conviction.

A grin takes over my face. "Yes, and I know how Trent works as well. I dated him too, remember."

Raine pauses and doesn't reply but just looks at me, those green eyes piercing into me. I have no idea what he will say next, so I quickly change the subject. "So, Tracy showed up on my doorstep today," I say, giving him a smile.

Raine looks down smiling and then he drops his silverware and grabs his glass of bourbon. He's uncomfortable, which is very uncharacteristic of him. It's sweet, but I still have my guard up. I must remember who I'm dealing with and why I'm here in the first place.

I continue, "Well, all I can say is, thank you. Tracy will be a big help. I'm having a hard time getting a meal outside of my room, so she can help with that," and I laugh a bit.

Raine nods in agreement. I pick up my silverware and cut into the waiting steak, which smells amazing and reminds me of home. There's a long, uncomfortable pause as we both focus on our meals, and I take a much-needed sip—more like gulp—of my Chardonnay. As I do, I notice my hand is trembling. I take a quick look at his face between bites and notice a dark look quickly cross his face.

"Are you okay?" I ask. "Is something wrong?"

"No ... no. I was just remembering one of the last times we had dinner together. It seems like yesterday."

My head drops down and I don't say anything before I look straight back up at him and smile. There's magic in the air and a sweetness between us, it's undeniable. But there's also a nervous tension like we both are worried we'll say the wrong thing. Earlier, I thought about Raine and that singer, Bethany, and it's silently playing in the back of my mind. I wonder if it will rear its ugly head.

Chapter Twenty-Two – Raine

I'm fighting my attraction to Julia throughout dinner. Luckily, we are seated, or I'm sure she would notice. It's all I can do not to grab her in my arms. When I opened the door, I was stunned. She looked even more amazing than she did wearing the long red dress for the show. The night has a light-hearted air I think we're both thoroughly enjoying. Finally, after finishing dinner and a couple of drinks, I turn the conversation back to something real. I can't help it.

"So, if there is nothing going on with Trent," I say with a slight pause, looking at Julia over the glass of bourbon I'm holding, "who are you dating?" I've always been direct. I calmly roll my glass of bourbon in my hands and wait for her response, intently watching her face. Julia looks at me and slightly rolls her eyes.

"I'm not really dating anyone right now," she says somewhat shyly, looking at me through her lashes. "When would I have time?" Then she nervously takes another sip of her wine.

"How did you end up back home?"

"I was offered a good job ... and honestly, I wanted to get as far away from Nashville, and you, as I could," she says quietly, her voice tinged with a sadness I can feel. "That town was nothing but heartache for me."

"Ouch. Well, can't say I blame you. I was an insecure asshole back then," I say, giving her a smile and watching her intently.

Julia picks up her glass of wine and laughs as she replies, "Most definitely. I'll drink to that." She's smiling, but there's truth in her words. Her next words are surprising, "It wasn't just you, Raine. I had given up. I missed music more than you could imagine, and I couldn't take living in a city filled with it and always standing on the sidelines. I gave up. It was my fault, I know that, but it was too hard."

I nod as she speaks, mulling her words over in my head. "I thought you dated some guitar player after me … what was his name?" I ask.

She looks at me, clearly exasperated, and pauses, looking away before replying, "I'm not going to tell you. I know how jealous you can get." She has a half-smile on her lips, but I know she's serious.

"Touché. It's better I don't know. I always told you: you and guitar players don't mix."

"You're a guitar player."

"That's different," I say, taking a drink. I know the conversation is making her uncomfortable, but I just can't help it. When it comes to Julia, I always push.

"What about you, Raine? Why aren't you with someone? You're handsome and successful. I figured you'd be married by now."

"No, darlin', I'm about as far away from married as I can get," I say before casually pausing to take a drink. "I haven't been able to get a certain brunette off of my mind," I add, nodding toward her. "Most nights I sit on my patio alone, feeling sorry for myself … and missing you." My tone is light, but I'm serious. I'm looking at her straight on, hoping she'll believe me.

Julia, obviously a bit stunned, quietly replies, "We just couldn't get it right, could we?"

I nod, take another drink of my bourbon, and lay it out there, "I know we need to stay away from each other, I don't want to hurt either of our careers, yours especially, but I mean it, Julia. I've missed you. Once this show is over, maybe we can try again?"

Julia looks down quickly, she's struggling with my words, that's obvious. "I don't know, Raine. What happened with Bethany. That was a lot to take."

And she did it, dropped the big elephant in this tiny room. I quickly reply, "What happened with Bethany was not what it seemed." I then stand and kneel in front of Julia, but I don't touch her, although that's all I want to do.

Looking right at her I continue, "Julia, nothing happened. I didn't sleep with Bethany. This may not make a difference, but I want you to know the truth. I passed out that night Bethany was at my house, and I have no idea how I even ended up in bed with her. Looking back, she probably tried to get me drunk, but I know one thing, I didn't have sex with her."

I look at Julia, but she's hard to read and her jaw is set. She's mulling my words over, and I can't tell if she believes me. I continue, hoping my words will convince her, "I wasn't myself back then. If I had thought that you would have listened or given me another chance, I would have tried to tell you the truth, but my head wasn't clear. I know I wasn't good to you. I was difficult and too demanding most of the time. I took you for granted and I should have been more careful."

Julia is still listening, watching me intently. Her arms are now lightly crossed with one hand holding her chin, like she is concentrating on my words, but her eyes are still set.

I continue, "When my head was clear, I tried to reach out and sent you a text, but you didn't want to talk to me. I get it. I wouldn't have wanted to talk to me either, but after all this time, I want you to know the truth. I didn't cheat on you."

Julia turns her head away from me and is quiet for several minutes, staring across the room. When she turns back toward me, she looks directly into my eyes, her own eyes glistening, and she says quietly, "I'm glad you told me. If you had tried to tell me the truth back then, I don't know if it would have changed anything. I don't think I would have believed you. I wasn't in the mindset to really believe anything you would have said at that point."

I nod as she continues, "Deep down I was angry with you. The years we dated on and off, we'd been through a lot. I was jealous of your busy career. I was always second and it seemed like I never really mattered to you. There were many times I felt alone sitting in the same room with you. You kept your distance and pushed me away so many times. I took it for a long time, but I couldn't do it anymore. I wasn't in a good place to take care of me and stand up for myself, but I'm taking care of me now. I'm putting myself first."

"Why did you agree to see me tonight?" I ask.

"I've tried everything I can to forget you. I vowed to hate you with every fiber of my being. I even moved hundreds of miles away hoping it would help, but my heart has never really let you go. I knew when I came to Vegas at the same time as the awards show, there was a chance I'd see you. And now that you are a part of the same show ... it's overwhelming."

My head is spinning, and it isn't from the bourbon. Right now, all I want to do is gather her in my arms and carry her over to the big, king-sized bed that's now looming in the other room. It's a good thing they gave me a suite and there's a wall separating us from the bed so I can't physically see what is so inviting in my mind. Earlier when I hugged her, it was like fire running through my veins, and now all I want is to see her in a state of undress in that bedroom.

But I want her to trust me that this isn't just about sex. Every word I said was the truth, and I truly hope she believes me. So, I do the safe thing. I reach out and grab her hands, which are now folded in her lap, and I lift one hand to kiss the top of it. Julia smiles down at me. I've got a chance, I think. After all this time, I still have a chance.

But this has clearly been too much, and Julia quickly stands. "I need to go. I've got an early day tomorrow," she says, stammering and grabbing her purse to leave.

"I understand," I say, but as she heads toward the door and out of my room I add, "I'm telling you the truth, Julia. I hope you believe me."

She looks back at me and nods as she opens the door, scans the hallway, and quickly leaves.

Chapter Twenty-Three – Julia

Conflicting emotions are raging through my mind. How Raine could work his magic on me so quickly, I will never understand. Inside my head, I was screaming, don't believe him, don't let him try to convince you he's telling the truth. He tore your heart out of your chest and stomped on it, remember? But my heart. My betraying heart listened to every word he said and wanted to believe it. In Raine's room just now, my heart was winning, as it always seems to take over when it comes to him. I forget all sense of reason.

I open my hotel room door and Tracy, who is lying on her bed with a pillow over her head, pulls the pillow away and looks at me with one of her serious looks.

"A good night?" she asks cynically. Tracy has known me for years and has been there through all the ups and downs I've had with Raine.

I walk over and slump down on the other bed. "Well, it was awkward at first, but I guess you can say it was good. Raine did a lot of talking," and my sentence falls at the end.

"Right ... you talked," she teases.

"It's not what you think, Tracy, really. It was a nice dinner, and he had the room decorated and everything. Basically, he said he wants to see me again, after the show is over, of course."

Tracy gasps slightly. "Wow ... and what do you think about that?"

"I'm not really sure," I say, pausing before continuing, "I sort of ran from his room, so I think it's up in the air. I'm still processing what happened. Raine seems different, Trace. I can't quite place it, but softer in a way. He's always been so gruff and, you know, kind of abrasive, but tonight he was sweet. I've never been around 'sweet' Raine before. He did tell me nothing happened with Bethany, that girl I found him in bed with years ago. Supposedly she got him drunk, and he was passed out that night. He says he didn't have sex with her."

"Do you believe him, I mean really? C'mon, he's a successful producer, rock star level. We both know what musicians are like. After everything that happened with Raine over the years, do you think he's telling you the truth?"

I look directly at my good friend as she lounges against the pillows, and it hits me. "I do. I believe him."

"Wow," she says with an incredulous grin on her face. "What now? What are you going to do?"

"I have no earthly idea," I say as I shrug my shoulders and sigh heavily. "But you should be proud of me. I didn't sleep with him. I didn't even kiss him."

"I *am* proud of you," she says sarcastically.

"I need a shower," I say, and I abruptly leave the room and enter the safety of the bathroom to be alone with my thoughts. The past few days have been a lot to take. One moment I'm back home, living a normal life, and the next I'm competing for a chance of a lifetime, and Raine is here, making my head spin and uprooting my plans. I would never have believed this was coming down the pike. I'm surprised at how easily I can accept his explanation about Bethany. I hope he's on the up and up. Maybe people *do* change? And even though I'm supposed to hate him, I don't. Except for maybe music, I realize that I love Raine more than anything else on this earth. I'm still hopelessly in love with that damn man.

##

I'm up early the next day reviewing the song lyrics in my head, over and over. Tonight, I'll sing the new song I wrote with Trent. He changed a few lines, so I'm doing my best to memorize them. I've got to get them right. I've had my phone at my side all morning and it buzzes. I jump a little when I look at the name. It's Raine.

"Thank you for coming to dinner. It was amazing seeing you and getting to talk to you again."

Again, I know I should play it cool and not send a message right back, but I'm always an idiot when it comes to him. I don't say much to him, "It was great to see you, too."

His reply, "Good luck tonight."

And that's it. I don't respond, because I don't want to say any more. My emotions are swirling. I must focus on the whole reason I'm in Vegas, not the man who so easily shattered me before and could easily do it again.

I decide to hit the gym to ease some of my tension. I have the day free until it's time to be at the arena. I wonder if I should run through my song again with Trent, but we're ready. I don't want to overthink it. Each pro writer will perform with their assigned contestant, and not only is Trent an amazing writer, but he also has one of the most beautiful voices in Nashville. I know we're ready.

I try to grab a quick lunch at one of the hotel restaurants with Tracy, but photographers and fans are everywhere, which makes me worry. It only takes one person to catch me with Raine or reveal our prior relationship and everything will be ruined.

Show time arrives quickly. I can have one guest backstage with me, and Tracy comes along. Members of my family have flown in for the show, and soon my father and my sister Jody will arrive, but I won't be able to see them until later.

As we walk into the green room, several of the female contestants are gathered in a group and I can see an iPad in one of the girls' hands. As I walk up, they all break away from me whispering. Aubrey walks toward me with her phone in her hand.

"Did you see this?" she asks. "Seems they have you and Trent in an amorous relationship."

I grab her phone, read a few lines of the online story, and then roll my eyes. Someone reported that I had dated Trent back in Nashville, and now a conspiracy is beginning to form.

I shrug it off. "It's nothing. We're just old friends."

Tracy looks at the phone and exclaims, "But look at how hot you two are." I glare at Tracy, and she just laughs. Aubrey agrees that we do look hot, so I take another peek. We do look good together, but my mind instantly goes to Raine. What will he think?

"Seriously, ladies, we're just friends," I say loudly for everyone in the room to hear.

I walk toward my dressing table trying not to let my anxiety show. So, a scandalous story has already started, but they picked the wrong guy. Thank God. Maybe this Trent dating story will distract the press from finding out about my prior relationship with Raine? It's a thought, and as I catch Tracy's eyes, I can tell she's thinking the same thing.

Chapter Twenty-Four – Raine

At the hotel, I'm on the phone with Bret.

"Sounds like Julia believed you about Bethany, and you two had a very responsible and grown-up evening. How boring," Bret jokes.

"Yep, too responsible," I mutter under my breath. Thinking back on our evening, I still can't believe I held myself back, when all I wanted to do was ravage her. The thought of her being in my hotel room with nothing intimate happening is a new one. Despite everything over the years, the want and need for sex overcame a lot of our relationship issues. Even if we weren't talking to one another, we could find our way around the bedroom.

"What?" Bret asks, breaking me out of my reverie.

"What time is our tee-time?" I say, covering my earlier remark.

"At ten … in just a few hours. Are you hungover? I'm not playing if you're hungover, you'll be an even bigger asshole than usual."

"I'll be fine, killer. Better bring your A-game."

I hang up and run a hand over my face. I didn't sleep much and although I'm beat, I'm filled with a positive energy I haven't felt in years. Before my dinner with Julia, I had no idea how the night would go, and I don't think it could have gone any better. Slowly, I'm going to win her trust. Show be damned, if I had to choose right now, it's no contest. Yes, this show will boost my career, but I'd rather have Julia. As soon as the show is over, somehow, I'm getting her to spend some time with me, and from the sexual frustration she left me with, it can't happen too soon.

##

After a terrible round of golf, I'm having lunch with Bret in the clubhouse. Bret has been trying to avoid the subject of Julia, but he's failing miserably. When Bret met me at the golf course, I'd already found Julia and Trent's story on my phone. Being from Nashville, it would've been hard to miss. Bret's been trying and failing to shake my bad mood.

"It's not true, Raine, you know it's not. Didn't she say they are just writing a song together. Nothing more."

"That's not what it says. Story says they've hooked up."

"Seriously? Do you think Julia has hooked up with Trent? That's ridiculous." Bret pauses slightly before continuing, "You know, maybe this is a good thing?"

I stop eating to glare at my friend.

"This may keep anyone from finding out about your history with Julia," he says.

"At this point, I don't care. This show is a mistake. I should just quit now, grab Julia, and take her to one of the wedding chapels here in Vegas."

"Okay, caveman, get a grip," he replies. "You deserve to be on this show and so does she. And do you think she'd give up that easily? She wants this."

I nod in agreement, but I grunt as an image of me trying to grab Julia and take her anywhere enters my mind. An image of her in a state of undress enters my mind next. "But look at the photo, Trent's hand is on top of hers. What's that all about?"

"It's taken out of context. Look, they're eating lunch. Julia has a salad in front of her. You can tell the photo was taken backstage at the arena."

I calmly nod, but deep down I'm pissed. It's in my DNA. I don't really believe what's depicted in the photo is true, but I can be jealous as hell. Even though Julia's not with me yet, I don't want her to be with anyone else.

Chapter Twenty-Five – Julia

An hour before the show starts, we're all backstage getting last-minute notes from the producers. Since they've kept the women in a separate area from the men, we haven't had a chance to interact with many of the guys. Based on the audience's reaction, a fan favorite is Jeremy. He's tall, blonde, and can really play the guitar. When Jeremy performs, screams fill the arena. Several of the other guys are also incredibly talented, and I wonder if a woman will break through and get the vote. I hope so, and I hope it's a forty-year-old country-pop singer.

They're going to mix up the show, and a female performer will follow each guy. My number is nineteen, and Jeremy is twenty. A coincidence? All I know is singing last never works for me because the chance that I'll actually vomit goes way up.

As the show starts, Katy Reynolds introduces our promos, and before each performer sings, they play a clip from a friend or family member talking about why they should move on to the next round. I give Tracy a skeptical glance.

"Wasn't me. Not enough money in the world would get me in front of that camera," she says dryly.

I wonder who they got to agree to film. It has to be a member of my family and all I know is that I can't watch, or I'll lose it and cry in front of everyone. The minutes drag as contestant after contestant performs. I keep getting up to pace around as Tracy watches with amusement. As they near number fifteen, my anxiety is in high gear.

"I think I need a shot of something," I say to Tracy. "I don't know if I can do this."

Tracy whispers to me, "Just sing to Raine. It's about him, isn't it? Just sing to him."

I nod and in a weird way, it calms me down. A few minutes later, I walk toward the stage as a makeup person fusses with my hair and gives me a last-minute touch-up. Again, I'm wearing more of a formal gown, but it's a light material and flows around me as I walk. It fits the mood of the song perfectly. Trent greets me at the side of the stage, looking calm and collected. He'll play piano and sing harmony.

After Katy introduces us, Trent grabs my hand and leads me onto the stage as the crowd erupts. I realize this will only add to the Trent rumor mill, but I let him. As soon as we reach the piano, I quickly drop his hand and move to the stand in front of the center-stage microphone. Through the lights, I scan the crowd and my eyes instantly look toward Raine. I can't see him, but I can feel his eyes on me.

Trent is all smiles as he looks at me, waiting for the go-ahead. I look at him, give a small smile, and nod. His fingers start the same melody I heard a few days before, and although I feel bare standing on the stage without my guitar, I let the music take me.

I hear a couple of catcalls from the crowd, and I smile just before I begin to sing. It's a different sound than the first night and it surprises the audience. The song called "Leaving Ashes" has more of a pop melody, and my voice is light and airy, but still strong and true. When Trent joins me in harmony on the chorus, the room is silent. I know we sound more than good together as we sing, "You've been bruised, you've been battered. You've crawled up off the ground. Like a phoenix you are rising, leaving ashes on the ground. You may be scared, you may be broken. You've had many bring you down. But like a phoenix you are rising, leaving ashes on the ground."

During the verses, I sing about failed attempts at life and love, but then finally getting it right, joining with your perfect person and rising above failure. I figure the crowd will think I'm singing about Trent, and this little song will add fuel to an already burning fire.

When we finish, Trent jumps up and grabs one of my hands, bringing it to his lips. I'm in shock but caught up in the moment of thunderous applause and cheers, and I don't react right away to his obvious affection. We walk together to the center of the stage to hear the judges' comments.

This time they start with Raine. Knowing how Raine feels about Trent, I'm more than concerned about his reaction to Trent's obvious affection toward me.

Katy turns to Raine. "Raine, what did you think about Julia and Trent's song?"

He pauses for a moment, looks down at a piece of paper before replying, "Truly an amazing song. They don't call Trent one of the best songwriters in Nashville for nothing. And I must say, vocally, Julia, I think that was better than your performance on Sunday. You should be proud."

I try not to overreact, but I smile broadly. Brandi and Davis give us similar remarks, and both comment on the strength of the song. Each song performed on this night will be immediately available for download following the close of the show. Some of the proceeds will go to charity, but some of the profits will go directly to each performer. They want us to make some money right away.

I walk off the stage with Trent and he leans in and hugs me, "You did it!"

I exclaim, "Trent, I can't thank you enough. I never would have had that response without you."

"I know how you can thank me. Have dinner with me when you're in L.A.?"

"I ... um ... I don't think that's a good idea."

"C'mon, what are you afraid of? Tabloids? Please ... it's just dinner?" he asks with those dark-brown eyes that will make a woman melt.

Tracy has walked out and is standing slightly behind Trent. From the corner of my eye, I can see Tracy nodding her head in a big "yes."

"Um, okay. I guess dinner would be okay, but someplace quiet and away from all the hoopla."

"I know just the spot," he says, smiling, and then he whirls away toward one of the producers of the show.

I walk toward Tracy, with my shoulders in a questioning shrug as I glare at my friend. "Why do you think that is a good idea?"

Tracy whispers, "It continues to keep any suspicion off Raine."

We walk back to the green room to join the group. At the end of the show, I meet up with my dad and sister. The show featured both in my video segment, and they're now minor celebrities. Then we all attend the after party. I do my best to stay clear of Raine physically, but mentally, he never leaves me. I catch him staring at me silently on more than one occasion, just as my eyes never really leave him as he walks around the room.

Chapter Twenty-Six – Raine

I'm standing with Bret at the after party, watching Julia out of the corner of my eye.

"Another home run. Your girl may win this thing," Bret says, nodding toward where Julia stands with her family. Bret is not about to miss a moment of the drama.

"It was good. Too good. If I score her too high, it could create more controversy if they find out we've dated."

"They won't find out, and if it's warranted, give her the score. You're doing the right thing."

"I am, but this could come back and bite us both in the you-know-what." I pause, picturing Trent and Julia on stage. "Did you see him take her hand and kiss it? Did you see him look at her at the end?" Obviously, I can't get their interaction off my mind.

I can practically hear Bret roll his eyes when he replies, "Julia hasn't been able to take her eyes away from you all night."

Just as Bret says this, Trent walks up to Julia's group and is shaking hands with Julia's father. A groan escapes from deep in my throat.

"Easy, fella, easy. Don't worry. I'm gonna watch that guy myself." Bret gives me a knowing look as he glares at Trent.

"I have never liked that guy," I say, and if my eyes were darts, they would have struck Trent in the back.

##

When I finally have a moment back in my hotel room, I send Julia a text, I

83

can't help it. I have Trent to contend with.

'Great song, you did well, Jules,' I write.

She responds back right away, 'Thanks for the kind words, they mean more than you know.'

'Can I see you … want to come up for a few minutes? Just to talk?' I know it's bold, and we shouldn't do it, but I want to see her. I start pacing around the room as I wait for her reply.

'Sure, give me 30.'

##

Thirty minutes pass, and I'm sure I've worn a path in the carpet from walking back and forth, anxiously waiting for Julia to arrive. I've changed into something casual, so I don't come across too strong. I hear a light knock and when I open the door, the Julia train hits me. She looks amazing in jeans and a black, off-the-shoulder blouse. She's taken off her stage makeup and her hair is pulled back. She looks amazingly fresh even at close to midnight and after singing for millions. Julia steps inside and just smiles. She seems different toward me in some way.

I can barely speak. "Glass of wine?" I finally say, gesturing toward the table where a bottle of Chardonnay is on ice. She nods, walks over, and puts her purse down on a chair. When she moves near me, her perfume floats behind, and it nearly knocks me over. It's one of my favorites, which I'm sure she remembers.

I walk over, pour two glasses, and hand one to her. She takes the glass and as she does her fingers lightly graze mine, sending shock waves through my body. I've been waiting eagerly for her touch, and I want more.

Julia takes the glass and walks over to the couch in my suite and sits, looking at me somewhat expectantly. So I grab my own glass of wine and sit down next to her. We don't say anything for a few moments, as she takes a sip before finally speaking. She's hesitant, you can hear it in her voice, and she won't look me straight in the face.

"I never really responded to your comment about starting a relationship again after the show is over." She pauses, and I just look at her sincerely, waiting for her to continue. She brought it up and I have no idea where she's going with this. Julia continues, "I've thought a lot about what you said about what happened that night with Bethany and everything, and I just wanted to say that I believe you. I believe what you said," and she turns away, nervously taking another sip of her wine.

I look down at her and smile before taking one hand and slightly turning her face toward mine, as I lean in and give her the softest kiss on those lips that have been calling me from the first moment I talked to her backstage after the first show. She leans in ever so slightly and I can feel her kiss me back tenderly. I pull back and smile, but I don't do anything else or touch her. She takes a long drink of her wine.

"Well, not much to do in here, do you want to watch some TV?" I ask, gesturing to the other room. I watch her eyes and they dart down for a second before she looks at me and nods in agreement.

We walk into the other room, and I go over to my usual side of the bed and set my wine glass down. I pick up the remote and flip on the flat screen, take off my Rolex, and then sit on the side of the bed to take off my shoes. When done, I relax against the pillows and just look at her. Julia has been standing in the doorway watching me, and then she walks over, puts her drink down, slips off her heels, and lays down next to me, her head resting on my shoulder with her hand on my chest. We're both still fully dressed. I let out a heavy sigh.

Although this may seem fast, we've known each other for so long it feels comfortable and right to have her next to me. She nestles into me as I flip the channels, looking for something mindless.

I finally land on a crime drama, and we watch in silence as I stroke her back lightly and she runs her hand across my chest. I'm sure she can feel every loud thump of my heart as I breathe her in. I'm lost in the sensation of her body against mine, which forms so well to my frame.

Julia finally speaks, leaning up to look at me, "Raine, when you sent me a text a few years ago, was it just to tell me about Bethany?"

I pause. "It was also around the time Bret and I had our first number one. I wanted to share it with you in some way. All those years ago, you knew how hard I'd worked to get there. I wanted you to know, I guess. You were always in my corner, and you never had an agenda … which is rare." My voice trails off.

She leans up to look at me. "I know the song you are talking about, and I knew it went to number one. I was happy for you, even though I hated your guts," she says with a smirk. "I don't mean to sound condescending, but I was proud of you. I'm still proud of you."

Julia settles back against my frame, relaxing against me, her head on the side of my chest.

"We didn't get it right back then, but maybe now is different," I say, as I absentmindedly run my fingers along her back. For now, I'm okay with just this. Of course I want more, but having her next to me again like this is worth every night I sat at home alone.

Maybe it's the wine at the after party or just being together after all this time, but as Julia strokes my chest, she finally speaks, her body tensing slightly as the words tumble out of her mouth. "I have missed you, Raine, more than you'll ever know. You may not want to hear this, but we're both older and life is too damn short … I still love you, I have always loved you, and I always will," she says, running her hand nervously across my chest. Her head is still down, not looking at me.

I take a short breath and my body tenses. I don't respond with words, but I pull her tight against me, and enfold her with both of my arms, as she softens back against me, tucking her head under my chin. It's my way of showing how much I care about her, even if I can't say it. For the first time in a long time, I feel at peace with her in my arms.

A few minutes later, Julia falls asleep, which is understandable since it's so late. I hear her light snore and I smile. My head is swirling as I hold this beautiful woman in my arms, my heart is light, and that's all I remember before I drift off.

Chapter Twenty-Seven – Julia

The next morning, I woke up entangled in Raine's arms. I got up and crept back to my room so no one would see me. Raine had to catch an early flight back to Nashville, and we've been texting all morning.

Later that day, I join all the contestants and board a flight to L.A. The following results show will be on Monday night, and four of us will go home. During the flight, I hear several other contestants talking about how worried they are about getting cut. I'm one of them, but I'm torn. Torn with wanting to stay and win it all, versus the hope of being with Raine sooner rather than later. I think about last night with Raine, and I can't believe it really happened. Just being in his arms was so amazing and so perfect. I'm kicking myself for telling him that I still love him, but I do. I couldn't help it.

I spend the flight contemplating all that has occurred, and what I should do. We arrive at our hotel, and I call Tracy, who has flown back home. I've already sent her several texts, so she knows about last night and what happened with Raine.

"If I get cut, might be a good thing," I say without mincing my words. I've had an entire plane ride with nothing to do but think. "I could then see Raine without any issue."

"Could you really?" Tracy asks. "I think you'd have to wait until things have blown over. If you two date right away, people will question him, and it'll create a shit storm for his career. And do you really want to give this up? You've worked your ass off, Jules. You deserve this."

"I know I deserve it, but I have another chance with Raine. People don't often get a second chance."

"If it's supposed to happen it will. Just be patient, which I know is not your strong suit," she says laughing at me. "So, what happens today, do you get to hang with celebrities or something?" Obvious sarcasm rolling from her lips.

"Oh lord … no, we just tape a couple of promos for the Monday night show. I'm free until then and I'll probably spend most of the time hanging out in my hotel room."

"Is tomorrow night the big dinner with Trent?"

"Yep, he sent me a text earlier today," I say with as much enthusiasm as if I'm heading to a root canal.

"You'll have a good time. He's a fun guy."

"But what if Trent thinks this is more than just a casual dinner between friends? It won't look right to Raine, I know it."

"Have you told Raine about your dinner with Trent?"

"No way, he won't understand. You know how Raine is … he is the most jealous man I've ever met. He will not understand me having dinner with Trent, not at all."

"You'll have to tell him something. You could frame it as you are trying to keep any speculation away from him, and Trent is a prop."

"Still won't work. Raine's going to be pissed. I know it. Not sure why I agreed to this, Trace, but Trent did say he would keep us out of the public eye."

##

Later that day after finishing my promos, I realize I have to tell Raine something about my dinner with Trent. If I don't tell him and he somehow finds out, it would make it worse. The last thing I want to do is spark his jealousy and lose what we've started to rebuild.

I send Raine a text, 'Hey, at the hotel room and thinking of you.' A few seconds pass and he calls.

"Hey there, I miss you," I say as he picks up. I can't help it; it just came out.

"Hey back … miss you too. What are you wearing?" Raine teases.

I give a nervous laugh, then pause. "Actually, I'm dressed for dinner. I'm heading out to meet Trent for a quick bite." I know we can't have any secrets, but I'm holding my breath as I wait for his response.

A long pause. Finally, he says, "Really, his idea or yours?"

"Trent asked … I'm sure it's just a follow-up to our song. It's no big deal, really. We're meeting at a low-key restaurant for dinner."

Another long pause. "Maybe it's a good thing? It may keep the media from uncovering anything about the two of us," he says calmly, but I can tell his teeth are clenched.

"What … did I just hear you right? You think it's a good thing?" I'm more than shocked as I look down at the phone in my hand, wondering who in the hell I'm talking to.

"I talked it over with Bret, and maybe you hanging out with Trent is a good thing. The press will hound you both and we can continue with the show. When the show is over, we'll give it enough time and then go public."

"I have to say I'm shocked … I never expected you to react this way. Tracy is trying to convince me of the same thing, which is why I agreed to have dinner with Trent."

"Then, it's all settled. Just send me a text when you get back to the hotel, so I know you're safe."

"I will. And really, Raine, it's nothing. Just dinner with an old friend."

"I'm trying to be mature about this, Julia. I believe you."

I hang up the phone not quite believing the conversation went the way it did. Wow. Raine never would have reacted this way years ago. Never. He's so different. Before, he never would have been so calm or so rational. It makes me smile as I realize the man I have always been in love with may have actually changed.

Chapter Twenty-Eight – Raine

I hang up the phone, walk over to my kitchen sink, pick up a glass, and almost throw it. But I calmly set it back down on the counter. I walk to the bar, pull a bottle of bourbon from the shelf, grab a glass, and start to pour, but again, I stop myself. These are my typical reactions. This is not the way to deal with this situation.

It was all I could do to stay calm on the phone with Julia. She needs to trust me and know that I can handle everything like a rational adult and not an insecure, jealous asshole, but my emotions are still raging. Damn that Trent. He's a slimy mother...

I pick up my phone and call Bret. "Meet me at the golf course in an hour."

"Can't, bud. Headed to the studio."

"Bret, if you value your life, you'll meet me at the course," I say through clenched teeth. "Julia is headed out to dinner with Trent, and I need to pound golf balls."

"On my way," Bret says with all seriousness.

I hang up and pour the glass of bourbon down the drain. Killing golf balls is a better solution.

##

At the course, I've never hit golf balls this hard. Bret watches with an obvious smirk on his lips. We opt to start on the driving range, and I'm like a machine. Bret chuckles as I drive another ball a good three hundred yards.

"When you are done with the show, I think you might want to take up professional golf," Bret jokes, watching a golf ball sail through the air.

I don't respond but grunt as I hit, or more like kill, another ball.

Bret asks, "Where is he taking her?"

"Don't know. Julia said it was a low-key restaurant, out of the public eye."

"Don't want to make this worse, buddy, but guaran-damn-tee-you, Trent is not taking her to a remote restaurant. He'll want cameras and fans. I bet this is more about his career and less about Julia."

"Well, either way, I'm gonna have one of the longest nights of my life waiting for her to text me. This sucks."

Bret doesn't respond but smirks and takes a long pull from his beer as he continues to watch me pound golf balls.

I return from golf ball bashing and spend hours in my recording studio. The thought of Julia on the town with Trent has sparked my creativity, and I can't put my guitar down.

Although a seeming relationship with Trent will keep focus off me and Julia, knowing she is out with Trent has me feeling completely out of control. I don't like it, not one tiny bit. Deep down, I trust her, but Julia has broken up with me before, probably because I wasn't treating her right, and she immediately started dating someone else. This is lingering like a cloud above me. I stop and scribble a few words down on my notepad and strum a couple of chords to match. At least I'll get a good song out of this as I continue to try and distract my mind from envisioning Julia with Trent.

Chapter Twenty-Nine – Julia

My car pulls up to the restaurant and as I peer out, I can see several photographers surrounding the entrance. As I climb out, the paparazzi scramble to get a shot. "Remote my ass," I mumble under my breath. I smile politely for the cameras as I fight to get inside the restaurant. Trent is waiting for me just inside the entrance and is dressed in a nice suit with an open collar. For a moment, I'm struck by how handsome he is.

"Sorry about the photographers ... I have no idea how they could have found out," he says to me apologetically, leaning in to give me a quick hug. "By the way, you look amazing."

I'm wearing a sleek black dress, not too short, but it accentuates my figure nicely. I'm self-consciously trying to smooth the dress down to cover as much skin as possible. I want to give Trent the benefit of the doubt, but I wonder if he has something to do with the photographers. The hostess leads us to a private table in the back. At least this part of his promise is true.

When we're seated and we've ordered our drinks, Trent turns and lightly touches my hand that is resting on the table.

"I'm so glad you agreed to join me tonight. Ever since that first show, I'd hoped we could spend some time alone. It's so great to see you."

I'm caught off guard and I just nod, thankful the server interrupts us with our drinks. Finally, I say, "Trent, it's good to see you, and I'm glad we got to work together, I truly am, but we are just friends. Good friends."

Trent nods, but he looks at me quizzically. I can tell he's hearing my words, but it's not registering. This is going to be a long night.

Trent continues to flirt with me during dinner and I'm polite, but I don't feel anything. Yes, he's a gorgeous man, but even with his "Sexiest Man Alive" good looks, he isn't Raine. I sit, trying to pay attention to Trent's words, but my mind drifts to last night and lying in Raine's arms. How I wish I were back there.

After dinner and another drink, I call my waiting car to meet me at the front entrance. I walk toward the exit with Trent, and just as we walk out the front door, he grabs my arm, pulls me to him, and plants a big kiss on my lips. Camera's flash all around us. I pull back, slightly shocked, not sure if the cameras catch this.

"Trent … I …what are you doing?" I whisper in his ear, which just makes us look more intimate.

"Julia, I know you want to be friends, but I want more," he says in my ear.

Trent turns and smiles toward the cameras as his hand drops to hold mine. We look like a new couple out on an intimate date, at one of the nicest restaurants in L.A. I groan but smile politely toward the cameras. I don't want to create a scene.

My car can't pull up soon enough and just before I get in, Trent pulls me in a tight embrace, planting another kiss on my cheek. As he helps me get in the car, cameras continue to flash.

"*DAMN!*" I say out loud after the car door shuts. I cannot believe Trent just did that! I'm absolutely furious as the car pulls away from the curb and I frantically search my purse for my phone. Kissing me in front of everyone …with cameras! Damn him! Raine is going to be more than pissed. I finally find my phone and call Tracy.

"Intimate and remote my ass, there were cameras everywhere, and Trent planted a huge kiss on me right in front of the restaurant. Trace, what have I done?" my angry, high-pitched voice squeaks out.

"It won't be as bad as you think, just give Raine a heads up. Let him know what happened."

But I cut her off, my anxiety rising with my words. "It wasn't a 'we're just good friends' kind of kiss. He planted a big one on my lips. What in the hell am I going to do about this?"

"Just tell Raine before he sees it on his phone."

I hang up and rest my head against the back of the seat. This is terrible. Raine will never understand what just happened. He won't.

##

On the way back to the hotel, I send a text to Raine, who I know is waiting to hear from me. "Just finished dinner and heading back to the hotel. There were cameras though, and they took pictures. Please don't freak out. Not true."

I eagerly wait for a response back, but I get nothing. I sigh heavily. As I glance out of the car window, I don't see any of the scenery before me and I'm completely sick to my stomach. All I want to do right now is catch a plane to Nashville. This is a hot mess.

I watch my phone the whole way back to the hotel, but I get nothing. I walk heavily into the hotel and up to my room. After a hot shower, I finally see my phone flashing and I run to pick it up. It's a message from Trent thanking me for dinner. I crawl under the covers and bury my head in the pillows, telling myself it will be okay, but tears stream onto the pillowcase. What if I lost my second chance with Raine because of this? He's so jealous, he may never forgive me. I check my phone for hours, but nothing.

First thing the next morning, I grab my phone and there's a voicemail from Raine. "I wanted to send a text right away, but I waited until I cooled down. I trust you, Julia, and believe this is all Trent. I didn't respond right away, and that was wrong. Have a good day today, sweetheart, I'll see you tomorrow at the show."

I collapse against my pillows, relieved, but staring at my phone. Who is this man and what happened to the real Raine?

##

Today, I'll spend most of the day working on my next original song. Even though I only get to perform if I'm not cut from Monday's show, I must focus on my music. It keeps my mind off Trent, stupid tabloid stories, and how much I miss Raine.

When I'm done rehearsing, I call Tracy, cutting to the chase. "Is the story

94

posted online yet?"

"Yep. One this morning and another about an hour ago."

"Boy … they don't waste any time, do they?"

"I must say, you look good, Julia, and, damn, Trent is one fine-looking man. If I weren't married," she jokes.

But I'm all business and still furious with Trent. "I only care about Raine's reaction, and he was great last night. He said he trusts me."

"See, I told you. I knew he'd understand. Who will be with you tomorrow at the show?"

"My family. Will be a fun time, and the pressure is off. I don't have to perform."

"And you'll make it through to the next round."

"I hope you're right; I really hope so."

I arrive back at the hotel and decide to order room service. I need a nice, relaxing evening to myself, away from tabloids and fans.

Chapter Thirty – Julia

After an incredibly long day, I'm now freshly showered with my hair up on my head in a loose bun, finally relaxing on my bed. My phone buzzes with a text from Raine, 'I'm here. I flew in a day early – I have to see you. Is that okay?'

I instantly respond back with my room number and Raine texts back he'll be up in ten. I don't bother to change out of the robe I'm wearing. We've known each other for so long, and he's seen me in various states of dress and undress. I realize just wearing a robe is bold, but the attraction between us is strong; it always has been. It's common for us to fall back into our old ways, I think with a smile. And I want him. I want this.

I hear his knock, and I open the door as Raine quickly walks in, closing the door with one hand, as his other hand pulls me tight against his frame, his lips grazing my forehead. My body trembles at his touch as Raine stands and holds me for a few moments. Without saying a word, I wrap my arms around his waist, and rest my head against his shoulder as he picks me up and carries me to the big, king-sized bed in the center of the room.

Raine puts me down on top of the bed and lies down next to me. His lips graze my neck and I shudder uncontrollably. He runs his mouth up my neck to my ear while his hand runs from my waist to my breast, as I lean against him hard.

"I like what you're wearing," he says, his voice gruff with desire, as I lightly chuckle.

His hand on my breast moves down my robe and opens it up, his hand grasping my waist pulling me tight against him. I can feel every ounce of him pressed between my legs and I start to pull at his clothes.

"I think you need to get rid of these," I murmur, pulling at his jeans as he slides the robe off my shoulders. I'm now half exposed lying next to him.

Raine stops and stands, unbuttoning his shirt as I watch. He continues to free himself of every stitch of clothing, kind of his own strip tease, and I laugh out loud as each piece of clothing falls to the floor. Our eyes never leave one another. By this time, my robe is gone, and my hair is down. He's watching my every move, his eyes devouring my now-naked body. He drops a condom he had pulled from his pants pocket on the nightstand, and then he lies back down next to me, running one hand from my ankle to my waist, his eyes following the trail. My hands go to his head, and as I run my fingers through his dark hair, and I softly pull him up toward my face, I want his lips against mine.

He moves his head up and his lips lightly graze mine, and then he comes back kissing me harder as he lightly pushes me back against the pillows, pulling his body up, and then down on top of mine. We're now fully skin on skin and it's glorious. His lips open mine and his tongue darts in playing with mine, and I lose all sense of control as he grabs my hair with one free hand and pulls, just a bit. It sends a jolt down my spine.

Raine stops kissing me for just a minute and says, "You are so beautiful." Then he leans back down and kisses me hard on the lips, and I respond back eagerly, my tongue mixing with his. He moves his mouth and runs his lips along my jawline and back to my neck. He's propped up on one arm and with his free hand, he runs his fingers up my upper leg and stops to eagerly press between my legs. Every nerve is on fire and all I want is to feel him. It's been too long. I moan with pleasure and reach out, clutching at his back as his mouth again finds mine. Raine presses against me hard, moving his legs between mine as I grip his shoulders. He's taking his time and it's taking me over the edge. I start to move against him. He stops for just a moment and grabs the condom.

"I had to go and buy these," he says chuckling, his voice deep in his throat.

I smile and tease him, "Sure you did, and hell froze over."

He grunts in frustration at my words. Once he is ready, Raine again rests his body on top of mine. He slides between my legs and presses hard against my wet, eager flesh. I reach a hand up to grip his hip, urging him on. He laughs deep in his throat at my insistence. He enters me with a practiced skill, and I moan with pleasure, my head thrown back. He knows my body so well and we fit together perfectly. He starts to move slowly as I reach up and grab his neck, pulling at him eagerly. One of his hands is underneath me, guiding my hip. Raine moves a bit harder, but is still taking his time, and while it's driving me mad, I'm loving every moment he's inside of me. Never missing a beat, he slides a hand up to my face and leans down to kiss me hard, plunging his tongue into my mouth, and I respond in kind gripping his hips with my legs.

I pull my face back and whisper, "Don't you stop … don't you dare stop."

"You keep that up and this will be quick," he mumbles with half-closed eyes.

I lean up, taking his tongue in my mouth as he grinds his hips against me, skillfully taking me to an even higher level of pleasure. I gasp and clutch his back with both hands, arching up toward him as he leans back to watch me. Sex between us was always amazing and we're carried to an even higher level, joined as one. I can't contain myself and exclaim out loud with each thrust of his hips. And as we have done many times before, we finish together, clinging to one another. Raine collapses holding me against him, his hands wrapped up in my hair.

A few moments pass and Raine leans up, careful with the weight of his body, as we catch our breath, still wrapped up in each other's arms and legs. He leans down and kisses me again softly on the lips before lying on his side next to me, with his head resting on his hand. He stares down into my eyes.

"Only one orgasm … you're supposed to have more than one."

"That was perfect," I say as I lean up and kiss him softly.

He smiles down at me, and then gets up and walks to the bathroom.

I watch him walk away and blush, my hand subconsciously coming up to my face. As I think about what just happened in my big bed, I could almost pinch myself. From my appearances on the show, to now making love with Raine, it's been one big, beautiful dream. I try not to think about the consequences of our actions, or anything other than the fact that Raine is with me right now, at this moment.

A few minutes later when he walks back toward the bed, I pull the covers back for him. He gets in next to me and pulls the covers up, tucking me in to make sure I'm warm. Something he wouldn't have thought about doing many years ago. He lies back and pulls me against the side of his chest, kissing my hair. We don't say anything for several moments. We're just enjoying being in each other's arms.

Finally, he says, "I'm sure I'm not supposed to ask you about this … in fact, I'm positive I shouldn't as I'm a judge, but your last song with Trent. Who was it about?"

"You really have to ask?"

"That's what I thought." Then he says quietly, "I really hurt you, didn't I?"

"Devastated comes to mind. You're the love of my life, Raine. What do you think?"

He doesn't immediately say anything, until finally, "Sorry doesn't cover it, does it?"

"It's a good start. A very good start."

He sighs loudly and pulls me tight against him as I rest my head on his chest. His hand is on my back and his fingers are lightly running up and down my spine.

"What are we going to do, Raine? If we keep sneaking around, someone is bound to see us."

"We just have to be careful. I don't care about me. It's you I worry about. We only have to do this until you are no longer a contestant."

I grow quiet, struck by his "no longer a contestant" remark. Does Raine think I will soon be cut from the show? I don't and can't ask, but his opinion matters more than anyone else on earth. Inside, I'm crushed to think he doesn't think I can win, but I try to put that thought out of my mind. I want to be fully with him now, in this moment, and not think about the show. Who knows when we'll be able to see each other like this again? I do know I can't wait until we can go public.

I stretch my body against his, breathing him in. I'm exactly where I'm meant to be, and I don't want to be any place else on earth. For the first time in a long time, I'm happy.

##

I wake up in Raine's arms and watch him sleep, snuggling closer to his body. He stirs and his arms, which are still draped around me, grasp a little tighter. I glance at a clock on the nightstand. He needs to slip out in a few minutes. It would be disastrous if someone sees him leave my room.

My mind goes to the night before. I'm reliving every moment, and I smile. He stirs again, half awake, and leans over to kiss me.

"I almost thought last night was a dream," he says, groggily. He stops talking, leans in, and kisses my lips.

When he stops, I say, "I can't stop thinking about it," and I pause to smile up at him before continuing, "But seriously, Raine, I don't want to stay away from you. I don't think I can."

"I don't want to be away from you either. We just have to be careful. Now that you're back in my arms, I'm never letting you go."

I'm quiet as he scoots down to be eye level with me. He leans in close and kisses me with such intensity, I can't breathe. We only have a few minutes until he has to leave, and we don't waste one moment.

Chapter Thirty-One – Raine

I lie awake, listening to Julia's steady breath as I hold her tight against my frame. I can't tell her, but I already consider her a favorite to at least make it to the top four. She could win this thing, although men typically win reality shows due to the voting demographic. It's not impossible but difficult for a female to win, and I want her to win.

Who would have thought I'd be where I am right now? I almost can't believe it. I have the woman I've wanted back in my arms, and I just have to make sure I don't blow it. Not an easy thing to do, I know that. Julia needs to really trust me, and I don't think we're there yet.

I softly stroke her hair, hoping my actions won't wake her, or maybe they will, and we can make love again. I truly can't believe how we found each other again and that we're both on the same damn television show.

I stare up at the ceiling and smile. Although I'm not sure how we'll maneuver this with the show, I'm in the best place I've been in for months. I'm happy. Truly happy.

Chapter Thirty-Two – Julia

I'm due at the arena by 10 a.m. for a quick rundown of the next show, lunch, and then I'm free until our 5 p.m. call for hair and makeup. My family arrived this morning and after lunch, we'll all hang out at a secure, reserved area by the pool. It will be a nice break before the stress of the big show reveal.

I can have four guests this time, so my dad, my stepmom, Jody, and her husband are all here. As we sit in the shade of a cabana, I watch for Raine. We casually discussed having him meet my family before the show. I'm glad they'll all meet in person, but we have to play it cool. Jody is the only one who knows we used to date. No one else will know they're meeting the love of my life.

From the corner of my eye, I catch Raine walk into the pool area. He doesn't walk up to our group right away but makes the rounds greeting other contestants and their families. He has Bret with him, and I stand as he approaches.

"Hi, Julia," he says as he shakes my hand. "And this is Bret," he continues, his eyes dancing as he gestures to his good buddy, introducing him like we haven't met before.

I put my hand out to Bret, but he opts for a quick hug, quietly whispering in my ear, "I'm pulling for you," and he quickly releases me, giving me a knowing, sly smile. I smile back.

"Raine, Bret, I'd like you to meet members of my family."

As I introduce each family member to them, I take special note of when Raine grasps my dad's hand in a firm shake and tells him it's good to finally meet Julia's father. My eyes are glistening as Raine makes small talk with my dad. Before they leave, Raine turns and gives me the slightest wink, and I can't help but give him the slightest smile in return, and then I glance around at everyone to see if anyone was watching. Luckily, our exchange seems to have gone unnoticed.

##

Later that day as I walk out of my hotel room, the hairs on the back of my neck go up. I look up and down the hallway carefully. I don't see anyone, but I don't feel like I'm alone. This ominous feeling stays with me all the way to the elevator. It's better when I'm finally in the safety of my car.

I'm finally able to shake the feeling during hair and makeup, and I'm cracking jokes with Aubrey like we're old friends. I'm so glad to have found a cool, down-to-earth person to hang out with. As the show opens, Katy Reynolds walks out on stage and the butterflies hit. I want to stay and give my career this chance. I deserve it.

After Katy's opening, all twenty of us walk out onstage. They'll introduce each contestant, and then the judges will add commentary about who they think should stay. It's all a blur as I look out at the arena full of screaming fans, family, and friends. As they announce my name and flash to my family, it hits me hard how far I've come down this winding road. Yes, at my age I'm an underdog, but each time I walk on that stage, I win.

After a short commercial break, they'll begin the torturous task of narrowing the field down to sixteen. I give Raine a glance, and I swear he smiles at me, but I quickly turn away. We're too obvious.

Katy walks back up in front of a monitor as we come back from break. "And in no particular order, I'd like to bring up the following five contestants. And one person from each group will leave *Next Real Star*."

Katy rattles off five names. I'm not in this first group but Aubrey is. One by one, Katy announces contestants who will stay or leave until they're down to just two standing by her side. When it's announced Aubrey will stay, I clap loudly for my friend.

After the next commercial break, a famous artist performs, and then the cycle begins again. They'll call up five performers, keep four, and then a celebrity or famous act will perform. Finally, my name is called in the final group along with Jeremy. I've been waiting, watching, and holding my breath and I'm surprised I haven't fainted at this point. I don't do well going last.

"And now, we're down to the final five of the night," Katy says.

You can cut through the electrified air as Katy announces the names. She announces the first two contestants who will stay. I'm not one of them. And now it's down to me, Jeremy, and Michael, a sixteen-year-old country singer.

Everyone in the arena is holding their breath, including me. I didn't know how much I wanted this until this very moment, and I have no idea how this will go.

"After compiling your votes with the judges' scores, America and our experts will keep ... Julia and Jeremy."

Thunderous applause surrounds us as I lean in to give Michael a hug and Jeremy does the same. I also give Jeremy a quick hug, and then we both wave to the crowd as the remaining other fourteen contestants join us on stage.

"Join us this Thursday night, same time, as each of the remaining contestants perform their next original song. Thank you for watching *Next Real Star.*" Katy signs off with a wave and the camera lights go black.

I look out at the judges' table and Raine is leaning back in his chair with his arms crossed, a satisfied look on his face. I know it's obvious, but for a brief moment, I smile openly toward him.

Backstage, we're all aflutter saying goodbye to the unfortunate four who are leaving. I walk up and give Aubrey a hug. I quickly gather my things and head out to meet up with my family.

Thank God we don't have a meet and greet tonight. I'm just going to hang out with my family, grab dinner, and relax. The next few days before the performance show are critical. The producers did let us know that a famous band will back each of the remaining contestants, like a mash-up with the contestant's new original song and one of the band's hit songs. Tomorrow, I'll perform my next original song acoustically for producers, and then they'll assign me to a band. No contestant will have a song mashed up with the same group.

As I walk out to my waiting car, my phone buzzes and I smile. It's Raine.

"Good night for you, my darling. Can't wait to hold you again. BTW – last night was AMAZING."

I climb into my car and quickly respond back, "Thanks, sweetheart. Can't wait to see you again."

I click off my phone and wearily settle back against the seat, relaxing for the first time all day. My car drives around and picks up my family and when they're in the car, they all buzz about the show.

When things settle a bit Jody leans in and whispers, "I noticed Raine smiling toward you. Has anyone mentioned anything about your prior relationship?"

"No, thank God," I whisper back.

"And what about Trent? What is that about?"

"Just some reporters trying to create a relationship when there isn't one." I don't add that Trent's also trying to put us into a romantic relationship without my participation. That's too hard to explain.

"Have you talked to Raine?" Jody asks. "What does he think about all of this?"

I debate letting Jody in on my secret but realize I have to wait a little bit longer. "He's cool. He wants me to do well. We don't want our prior relationship to create controversy and bite us in the ass."

In the back of my mind, I know that is exactly what might happen.

Chapter Thirty-Three – Julia

Later that night, I open the door with a smile as big as Texas. At this moment, I don't care about any consequences, just that Raine is standing before me. He slides inside the room and grabs me into a tight bear hug, burying his face in my neck.

"Damn you smell good, and feel even better," he says against my hair.

When he sent me a text that he was coming to my room, hell or high water, I quickly changed into a flimsy black negligee and platform pumps.

I press myself against him. "But you haven't said one word about what I'm wearing."

"Very nice, but you won't be wearing it long."

I laugh as he picks me up and carries me to the bed, and with one arm he lays me down, while his other hand struggles to remove his pants and shoes as I lean up and tug at his shirt. I slide it up over his head giving him a disheveled look, which matches his level of passion. He quickly rests his hard body on mine, grinding his hips against me. He slides my negligee up and once it's gone, he runs his hands down the front of my body, his lips following his movements. I moan with every touch of his lips.

"Damn ... I've missed you," he says under his breath.

"It's basically just been a day," I say, exasperated but laughing at the same time.

I pull his face up and kiss him hard, and then he moves his lips to my neck while I reach for a condom on the nightstand. Even though we're impatient, we have to be practical. My arms go around his shoulders and I pull him tight against me. Once he's ready, he enters me quickly, leaning up to watch my response as he buries himself within me as deep as possible. Instantly my legs wrap around his hips. We're both impatient and quickly lost in one another, neither saying a word but carrying each other to a level of ecstasy we have found so many times before. Raine does everything he can to hold back as he watches me reach a higher level of bliss.

Raine holds me tightly against him never taking his eyes from my face. I grip my hands behind his neck, bringing his face to mine time and again as we kiss long and deep. It's like we haven't made love in years. After I come hard the first time, Raine rolls over pulling me on top of him. I lean back and he watches me use him for pleasure as he holds onto my waist, his eyes savoring every ounce of my body as I move forward and back on him. My tempo increases and after I reach release again long and hard, he rolls me onto my stomach, fluidly sliding between my legs, his hands guiding my hips.

Raine's thrusts increase, moving hard and deep as I stretch my arms above my head, clenching the sheets with every move he makes. We're both lost in the sweet sensation of being one. Raine's movements are now coming faster and deeper as he takes a hold of my hair in one hand, gently pulling back as I gasp and moan with every thrust.

It doesn't take long for us to finish together this way. When we both catch our breath, Raine rolls to his side and pulls my back tight against his body. His arm holds me in a firm, protective grip as I rest against him. We don't speak and we don't have to. The world could crash down around us, and we wouldn't care.

##

Raine holds me tight all night and the few times I do stir, he grips me tight against his body, whispering softly into my ear. I've slept soundly all night against him, his touch soothing and the sound of him sleeping next to me like a relaxing drug.

Raine is in the bathroom when I finally wake up. As I stretch my arms above my head, my hands hit a small box lying on the pillow next to me. I pick it up just as he appears in the doorway, watching. I look at him quizzically, and his right brow rises as he nods toward the package but doesn't say a word. There is a small note attached to the box, and my eyes raise up to meet his as I open the note.

"I can't wait one minute more. This is not as beautiful as you, but for now, it's our symbol of what's to come. I love you." I give him a sideways glance, and then gasp as I open the box, my eyes focusing on the ring inside.

He quickly walks toward me and kneels by the bed. "What do you think? Will this work?"

"Will it work?" I say laughing. "Oh Raine … it's gorgeous."

Raine takes the box and pulls the ring out, and then slides it on my ring finger. It's a platinum band with alternating black and white diamonds. And the center emerald cut diamond stone is breathtaking, but not garish and it suits me perfectly.

"I've never said this before, and I'll never say it again. Julia, I want you forever, every day, through anything put before us. I love you more than life, and definitely more than this dang show."

I look at him and my eyes dance.

Raine continues, "Marry me. When all this show bullshit is over. I want you to marry me."

I pull him tightly to me as tears well up in my eyes. I pull back and just nod.

"I take it that's a yes?'

My breath is ragged, "Yes. It's yes. When all this show bullshit is over," I say laughing.

"Those are the most beautiful words you have ever said to me," he says, a full grin filling his beautiful face, which looks perfect with his messed-up jet-black hair. He kisses me hard and I pull him down on top of me as we celebrate our engagement the best way we know how.

##

I shower and walk to my bedroom mirror, staring silently at the woman standing in the reflection. Never before have I been so happy. Since we have to hide our engagement, I slide the ring off my finger and walk over and put it in the safe in my room.

Raine dressed and went up to his room before 4 a.m. I had told him about my creepy feeling, like someone is watching me, and he didn't want to take any chances.

Later that morning, there's a knock at my door.

"Room service."

"Um … okay. Just a moment." It's a bit odd they're at my door this early, but maybe they are picking up the dishes I didn't leave in the hallway.

I throw on some sweats and pull my hair back before heading to the door. I had cleaned up my plates from yesterday and have them stacked on a cart that I roll to the door. I look through the peephole and a hotel staff person is standing there. I unlock the door and open it wide, just as a bright light flashes in my face.

"What the? What are you doing!" I yell as a man runs off. I quickly slam the door shut with both hands and flick the lock, my chest heaving. What the hell just happened? My creeped-out feeling was spot on. Someone is watching me and trying to catch me with someone. But who? Raine or Trent?

Chapter Thirty-Four – Raine

As I'm walking out my hotel door headed to the airport, my phone rings. It's Bret.

"Yes?"

"I knew she'd move on to the next round," Bret says knowingly.

"Yep." But I don't say any more about it to him. I'd scored her well, but I'd also been fair, and I don't want anyone, even my best friend, to question my integrity.

"Next show is Thursday, right? Are you staying in L.A., or are you headin' back to Nashville?"

"I have to meet with a label in Nashville, so I'm flying out this morning. Then back out here late Wednesday night. I didn't realize how much work it takes to juggle the show and my real-life career."

"Are you writing any new songs?"

"Wrote a hit the night Julia had dinner with Trent."

"I'm sure. I already want it, so hold it for me. I'm sure it's a good one."

"Definitely."

"Have you talked with her, and what was up with you meeting her family the other day?"

"I had never met them before," I say, trying to avoid his questions.

"Uh-huh. What are you not telling me?"

"Just that one day we'll make it permanent."

"Dang—seriously? That's why you were so nervous. Dude, I'm happy for you, and for Julia."

"Be happy, but don't say a word."

I grab my suitcase and walk to my waiting car. I really didn't want to head back to Nashville, but I can't have Julia so close. I can't control myself with her so near.

Chapter Thirty-Five – Julia

First, I sent a text to Raine letting him know someone had posed as room service and snapped a picture. Now, I have hotel security on the phone and I'm telling them about what happened.

"You're sure it was a photographer?" the man on the other end asks.

"Definitely a professional. A fan or even a stalker would have stayed. This guy ran off," I say to the hotel staff.

"We'll put someone outside of your room immediately."

I then reluctantly call one of the show's producers to let them know what happened. Although I'm sure it was paparazzi trying to get a shot, I can't take any chances in case someone is stalking me. I quickly get ready so I can get out of the hotel. Hotel security also wants to put me in a different room, so I throw all my stuff in my suitcases, and remembering the ring in the safe, I grab it and stash it in my purse.

Later, I'm climbing into my waiting car, just trying to breathe, but my heart is racing. Great. My first day working on my new song and I'm a total wreck. My phone buzzes with a text from Raine.

'Are you, okay?!? I need to get additional security for you.' He's frantic, that's easy to tell.

I send a brief text back, 'I'm okay. Just startled. I'll send you a message later when I'm done rehearsing. Everything is fine.'

But I'm not fine. I'm completely drained, not only because of the stalker-like photographer, but at what I fear they'll find or already have proof of. They won't stop until they have plastered images of me all over and destroyed my new career, and likely Raine's career, too. Suddenly it hits me how hopeless this is. There probably isn't any way out of this.

Chapter Thirty-Six – Raine

I'm nervously pacing around the airport lobby. Julia was right. Someone is following her. *"Damn it!"* I exclaim. For the rest of the show, I can't be seen alone with her at all. Too risky.

I text Bret before boarding my flight, 'Someone, a pub, found out something about Julia and tried to get a picture of her in her room. Can you try to find who's behind this? It's time to use all the connections you have. This is not a joke.'

Finally, a message back from Bret, 'I'm on it. I'll call you later to get more details.'

I board the plane and plop heavily into my seat, running my hand through my hair, and down my face. I'd already been worried someone was going to find out about us, and now I'm worrying about Julia's safety. First and foremost, I want her safe, but there's no way I can call the hotel and demand more security for her. It'd be odd for a judge to call about a contestant. I have to let the show staff handle it.

I stretch my already cramped legs and the first thing I do is order a double bourbon. This is going to be a long flight. I can only hope Bret finds something out. I have never been more helpless in my life, stuck with nothing to do and no way to help.

Chapter Thirty-Seven – Julia

I'm jumpy when I arrive at rehearsal, and it takes everything I have to rise above my scare. I'll perform my song acoustically for the producers, and then I'll find out what act I'm partnered with. My adrenaline is soaring. In my gut, I know it's only a matter of time until my name is mixed with Raine's and plastered all over the media.

After playing for the producers, I have time for lunch. As I reach my waiting car, someone yells out my name. I jump at first but calm down when I look back and see Trent walking toward me.

"Hey girl. I had hoped to hear from you after our dinner, but I got nothing," Trent jokes, a grin filling his face. His bright sky-blue eyes cause me to catch my breath for a moment.

I'm still miffed at Trent for the other night at dinner, but due to our working relationship and the fact that we were friends, I'm polite. "Well, I have been a little busy," I say, pointing at the rehearsal hall. If he only knew.

"Oh yeah, right, the show. It's always something," he says teasingly, moving closer, which is more than a little disconcerting. "How about we grab a quick lunch?"

I hesitate. "I don't know, Trent. The last time we shared a meal, there were more pictures taken of us than when a royal prince gets married." I'm subtly trying to let him know I'm not interested. I don't need anything else on my plate right now.

"True … but this time, I know this really intimate place."

"I'm sure you do," I say sarcastically. By now my driver has the car door open, and I have one foot in the car. I know I should go, but I hesitate. "Let me guess, only a few photographers?"

"How about none? I have a house here in L.A. I could whip us up a quick lunch."

I pause and Trent presses, "C'mon, it's no big deal. It'd be good to talk with you again. I miss Nashville and it helps by talking with you."

My gut is telling me no, but he's relentless and, in a way, I feel sorry for him, "Okay. A quick bite, but I've got to be back here in a few hours."

Trent nods as I look at my driver, who has been watching and waiting to see what I'll do, and I nod at him. I close the door and walk toward Trent's BMW. He opens the passenger side door for me before walking around and sliding into the driver's side seat. We snake through the streets toward Beverly Hills, making small talk.

We pull up his drive and as I get out, I look around at the grounds. He must have done well with his songwriting, or at least invested wisely. It's a large, sprawling estate.

"So, you have this house, but you still have a home in Nashville?" I ask as we walk toward the house.

"Yep. I've been working with some pop and rock acts here and it makes sense. I got tired of living in hotels."

"I know what you mean, but you can't beat room service."

"True, but I like to cook."

"I never knew that. What are you going to make us today?" I ask, warming up a bit. At least Trent is helping me forget about my morning photographer scare.

"Nothing too fancy, but it'll be good," he says with that Texas drawl as he gives me one of his gorgeous smiles. It's not hard to find him attractive.

We walk in and Trent shows me around the main level. He has his own workout room and several bedrooms. Out back, a graceful pool fills the backyard, and he also has a small guest house with a recording studio on the property.

He makes us a fresh salad, all organic, and a juice concoction filled with strawberries and bananas. For the fresh food alone, I'm glad I joined him. We relax on his patio talking easily.

"Seriously, I hoped you'd call after our dinner," he says.

"About that ... laying one on me in front of all the photographers. Really, Trent? Did you plan that?"

"Nope. Just happened. I like you, Julia. I'm sorry. Maybe it was a bit strong, but I don't have time to play around."

I pause, then decide to spill some of my secret, just so he'll get the hint. "Trent, you're a great guy, but there is someone I'm seeing and it's serious."

Trent leans back and eyes me with a smirk. "I thought so. There aren't too many women who can withstand my charm and charisma."

"And you're humble, too," I say sarcastically.

"Yes, there is that." He smiles and picks up his juice glass as he says, "To a beautiful lady, inside and out, who I unfortunately can't have."

I laugh as I lean in and touch my glass with Trent's.

Chapter Thirty-Eight – Raine

Although I secretly already know, the show's producers brief me about Julia's run-in with a photographer, and I act like I'm shocked. We're all now required to take extra precautions. When I get back to L.A., I'll have additional security, which will make it even harder to see Julia.

I finish up a meeting in Nashville, and then I'm headed home to pack when my phone buzzes. It's an email from the show's head producer.

'We've assigned the bands with each contestant. List is attached.'

I eagerly open the attachment and search for Julia's name. They've put her with Flashback 40, one of today's hottest bands, with a lead singer who often frequents the cover of magazines "Great." I groan out loud. Flashback 40, another hot singer. I'm glad for her and I'm sure they'll be amazing together, but *seriously*! I think about sending her a text, but I don't want to spoil the surprise.

As I'm driving to the airport, Julia calls and she instantly fills me in, "Did you hear? Flashback 40. Holy shit!"

"I did hear. Are you trying to kill me?" I can almost hear her smile through the phone.

She teases me, "Now who is the lead singer of the band, I don't remember his name?"

"Sure, you don't. Well, according to several magazines, he's one of the sexiest men alive."

"Oh yeah ... that guy," she says laughing. "I guess I'll need to be on my guard then."

"And I need to go out and hit golf balls," I say under my breath.

"What? What about golf balls?"

"Nothing ... I'm in tomorrow, late." Although I know we shouldn't see each other after what's happened, I push, "Can I come up to your room?"

"Raine ... I don't know. After today's room service incident, I think we'd better play it cool."

I pause because I can hear it in her voice, she's backing off and suddenly a sharp pang hits my chest. "Okay, I get it. Well, I'll send you a text when I get there."

"That'd be great. Yes, let me know when you arrive safely."

And that's all she says. It was almost cold at the end, and I have this pit in my stomach that's reared its head before.

##

The next day, I have a few radio and press interviews for the show before I need to catch my flight. I spend most of my time at the airport and between flights, I'm managing details of my life back in Nashville when halfway through the day, I notice Julia hasn't sent me any texts. I try not to think much about it, but it's there, weighing on me. I seriously wonder if I should just pack it up and, citing personal reasons, withdraw as a judge. I don't want to end up losing her, not over this. I want to see her move on and even possibly win the show.

Bret calls me as soon as I land in L.A. "You're not going to believe this."

"Lay it on me," I say back with dread. I can tell by his tone this is serious.

"There's a rumor that Bethany, your former background singer, called a tabloid. It's just a rumor, but I'd bet money on it."

"Makes sense. Bethany knows I dated Julia. I'm not surprised," I reply as calmly as possible. "I'm going to drop out as a judge. Julia wouldn't be in this position if I weren't a judge, and I want her to have the opportunity to win. I already have a successful career. She deserves the right to live her dream, which is to write and sing."

"I understand, buddy, but there is no way I'm letting you drop out."

"I don't see any other way?"

"Don't do it. Somehow this will all work out," Bret says before we end our call.

I click off my phone and realize not only could I lose her, I'm also consumed with her safety. I let out a heavy sigh. At least now we know who the source is. That takes some of the edge off, but if I do drop out, does it solve the issue? I'm not so sure. Even if I'm free from the show, if the press finds proof, they'll have a field day.

##

Later that day, Bret confirms that Bethany is the initial source. Bret has also heard an L.A. photographer has personally witnessed me coming out of Julia's hotel room but has not captured a photo. The early morning room service ruse was the attempt to catch us together. I'm getting more and more pissed with each of Bret's texts. There must be some way we can come clean and redeem ourselves. I've got to come up with something. Bethany wants revenge and she won't stop until she has it. At the moment, it looks like Bethany is winning and I'm losing the one thing that really matters.

Chapter Thirty-Nine – Julia

After an exhausting day, I walk to my bed and pick up my phone. There's a single line text from Raine, 'We think Bethany leaked to the press.'

I sit on my bed, looking down at the little black phone that will likely destroy my life and career. Once the news that I've dated Raine hits social media, I'm done. I have never felt so defeated. My relationship with Raine could ruin any chance I have to live my dream. And not only that, but it also seems like every time I'm with Raine, something happens so that it never works out. I call Tracy, who picks up right away.

"Did you see the trash mags today?" Tracy asks before I can get a word out.

"No … I haven't," I reply quietly.

"They have more pictures of you and Trent at his house. They have pictures of the two of you entering his house, eating lunch on his back deck, and leaving together in his car."

"Really? That may be the best news I've heard all day."

"What? Why?"

"Someone faked being with room service and got a picture of me in my room, shortly after Raine left. We're sure it was paparazzi, but luckily, they didn't get us together. The jig is up and I'm going to quit the show. There really is no other way out."

"My ass, you're gonna quit! No way. Why do you think it was a pro photographer?"

"They ran off and it makes sense, and we've heard Bethany, the girl I found in Raine's bed years ago, tipped them off. There's nothing else I can do but quit. Once this comes out, my career is over. I've got to bow out before shit hits the fan."

"There must be a way," she says trying to lighten things up. "By the way, you and Trent do look hot together. Damn, he's a good-looking man."

I can't help but laugh at her obvious Trent crush. "Yes, he is, but now they are going to say I'm seeing them both. This sucks."

Tracy spends a few more minutes trying to change my mind. We agree that I'll stay and perform during the next show, and we'll see what happens. The one thing we can agree on, I cannot see Raine at all. Too risky.

The show's producers sent a copy of my song to Flashback 40, so they're familiar with it. I have no idea what song the band will choose to mash with mine. At a time when I should be so excited for this next step, I can't eat, and deep, dark circles under my eyes relay the kind of night I've had. Although the intimate nature of my relationship with Raine isn't necessarily wrong, in the eyes of the world it's a breach of trust. I must end all contact with Raine, Trent, and any distractions and focus on the show. My career and my reputation depend on it. If I lose my reputation, I'll lose everything.

At the arena, I greet Flashback 40 and we make small talk as I mask my inner turmoil. They'll mash my new original song, "Start Over Again," which is an up-tempo pop-flavored "done me wrong" song, with their latest hit single, "Stop Sign." When I first meet the band, I'm starstruck by their lead singer Andy Mitchell, but he's cool and down to earth. We rehearse for several hours until we finally feel like we're about there.

My extra security greets me at the stage door, and they walk every step with me to my car. While in my car, I try to relax against the seat, but I can't shake the feeling that I've done something wrong. Do I really deserve to be a competitor on this show? It seems like too many things are stacking up against me. Maybe it's a sign?

All I want to do is get back to my room and try to relax. A nice, hot bath and room service will help. So would a visit from Raine, the one person I want to see, but I have to stay as far away from him as possible.

##

The next day, I have a final rehearsal with Flashback 40, and then I'm buried with promo photos for an upcoming *People* magazine article. The show's different approach, original songs, and driving votes to social media are paying off. The ratings for the first two shows are through the roof. Keeping everyone's identity a secret generated so much buzz, the show has been trending on Twitter for the past few weeks.

Of course, my rumored relationship with Trent is trending high on Twitter as well. Whenever I'm around the other contestants, they get quiet. Some look at me with disdain that I'm getting press, but they can have it. I don't want it. Only Aubrey acts like nothing is up and treats me normally.

When I'm finally safely escorted to my room, I call Raine. He picks up on the first ring.

"Hey, darlin'," he says. "Busy day. Yours?" I can tell he's trying to be light.

"Yes, rehearsal with the band, an interview, and photos. Exhausting, but not what is on my mind. I've decided I'm going to quit after this next performance show."

Raine quickly replies, "Like *hell* you're quitting. I'm leaving as a judge. I've decided to tell the producers immediately after this next show they'll have to find someone else. Then you can continue."

"I don't want to continue. Bethany wants to get back at you, Raine, and she won't stop. The publications won't either. If I leave, we can put the blame all on me and you can salvage your career."

"I don't care about my career and no matter what, I'll be fine. You're not quitting. I repeat, you are *not* quitting!"

"Let's change the subject. You haven't asked me a thing about Andy Mitchell," I tease.

But Raine doesn't bite. "Don't care. You are not quitting," he replies, his voice firm.

I know he won't drop it unless I relinquish, so I tell him I'll think about it. But in my mind, there is no other way out.

"By the way … I miss you," he says, and I can hear him sigh on the other end. "You have no idea what that photographer has done to me. I'm a wreck.

I can't do anything to protect you."

My heart stops for a moment, picturing his nervous energy getting the best of him. I don't say anything and Raine continues, "I just want you safe. Nothing else matters."

"I am safe. You're a couple floors away and if anything happens, I can run right up," I tease, but then I turn serious. "Raine, we know Bethany won't stop, so it's best if we don't see each other or anything. If I'm on this show, even just for one more performance, I have to stay clear. I don't need any other questions about my integrity."

Raine is quiet for a few moments before finally saying, "Julia, you do know I want to marry you, right? We can both quit right now and go back to Vegas and do it. To hell with what anyone thinks."

"Isn't there a song about that?" I lightly tease but then I continue, this time in all seriousness, "Maybe this is all too hard for us? Maybe this is a sign we need to just stop?"

I hear his intake of breath and then silence. "Raine … are you there?" I ask.

"Is this about Trent? Are you seeing him?"

I can't believe he went there. "No! I'm not and you know it. You're always *so* jealous," I say, my voice rising. "This is why it's so hard for us to make this work. The timing is always off, and things happen, like Bethany. Maybe it's just not meant to be? Even if one of us leaves, there will still be questions."

"Fuck questions," he says so quietly I can barely hear him. He's more than pissed. Raine continues, "You're just scared. Scared when it gets too hard. Scared of failure and scared that you'll get hurt. That's all this is."

Then he hangs up the phone as I stare at it. I think about his last words and how they are probably right on the mark.

##

Show day comes with a vengeance, and I'm booked solid. Although they've officially released the news that each contestant will sing with a famous band, the pairings are kept confidential, creating a new surge of social media buzz.

I'm at the arena early to prepare. The show won't start until seven, but we have to run lighting and sound for each of us with our band. The two-hour show needs to run like clockwork. I also have several segments to tape for the following Monday night's show.

By five when I'm sitting for hair and makeup, exhaustion is seeping into every bone. This, coupled with tossing and turning all night thinking about Raine, and I turn to coffee to make it through the next few hours. Once I'm done with this performance, I can focus on how I can leave the show with as little damage as possible.

I've exchanged many texts with Tracy about everything. She agrees with Raine that I'm just scared, and I probably am. But I have every right to be scared. Raine's hurt me so many times that when it feels too hard, it might be best to walk away.

As I head from makeup to the green room, I catch Raine sitting in a chair, with his pretty makeup artist chatting him up, and I watch him laugh with her. He doesn't see me, thank God. Seeing him with another woman, like he doesn't have a care in the world, only reminds me of how he can be a careless asshole.

I must focus on what I have to do. Performing with Flashback 40 should be one of the highlights of my career. I need to focus on that and stop thinking about Raine.

Chapter Forty – Julia

A few minutes before show time, surprisingly, I get a text from Raine. 'I've heard your performance with Flashback 40 is exceptional. Good luck. You deserve to be here.'

I drop my head and silently pray for the strength to match the talent of the band, and for the wisdom to do the right thing. I'll perform during the middle of the show, number eight out of sixteen. Due to the length of the show, they've cut our mashed-up song to three and a half minutes. The timing has to be perfect, so at the last minute, we've cut some of the song. I have to get it together. I cannot mess up on national television while singing with Andy Mitchell. Young girls across the country would never let me live it down.

The show starts and again, we all surround the large TV screen backstage. Katy Reynolds looks amazing, and when they flash to Raine, he looks tired, but as good as usual. He's less formally dressed in a tight shirt, black jeans, and boots. He walks out to his seat, waving to the screaming fans.

"You ready, girl?" Aubrey asks me.

"Ready as I'll ever be. Can I ask now as we are about to go live, who are you singing with?"

"The Blue Tones," Aubrey replies with all seriousness, but she has a wide grin on her face.

I gasp 'cause it's one of the biggest rock bands of all time. "No way … wow. That's amazing!"

"I know. I've had to pinch myself every day. And you?"

"Flashback 40."

"You're kidding ... is he as hot in real life?"

I give her a knowing smile, "Hotter."

Aubrey laughs out loud. "You're lucky," she says, patting me on the back. She picks up a bottle of water and hands one to me. "Here's to two of the luckiest women on the face of the earth."

I smile and raise my water bottle in a mock toast as my stomach turns. After the past few days knowing about Bethany, a persistent photographer, and the fact that my whole world could completely crash down, I don't consider myself lucky. We stop our conversation as they start the countdown on the big screen.

I watch the first few performances in amazement. Aubrey performs fourth and wows the crowd. The entire Blue Tones Band, now all in their mid-sixties, still have it. So far, all the performances have been stellar. I don't know if my song will stand up to what I'm seeing and hearing.

When it's time to hit the stage, I stand in the wings and wait. They've dressed me in a short black dress and tall platform boots. It feels different and fun, and from a pure performance perspective, I can't wait, but I'm terrified. I have to make Andy and Flashback 40 look good. I don't feel pressure for me but for them. I must be flawless.

As they call my name, Andy takes the stage and belts out the first line of "Stop Sign" and the crowd erupts. I wait until it's my time to join him on stage, and then walk out singing the first line of my song, *"Oh, what to do, when a liar, he takes hold of you."* Andy looks at me and smiles, and suddenly all my tension is gone. I walk toward him as he joins me in harmony. We sing a few lines to my song, and the band plays perfectly. Then we switch to the chorus of "Stop Sign," and I join Andy in harmony. I'm standing right next to Andy, and then we turn toward each other. I almost mess up one word of their song, but Andy mouths the words at me.

We switch back and forth between the two songs, and as I used to be a dancer, I'm moving easily on stage but not as well as Andy. He's amazing. Toward the end of our performance, we turn in unison and walk out on the ramp that leads into the crowd. Singing along with Andy is a surreal moment.

I realize how lucky I am as I turn toward the crowd and smile. We finish the song side by side, looking at one another and hitting the final notes perfectly. A moment of silence hits us, followed by a thunderous eruption from the crowd. The rest of the band walks up and joins us at the edge of the stage as the audience and judges all give us a standing ovation.

Each judge raves about our performance. My gut tells me we've hit a home run. The rest of the performances are all amazing in their own way, but another performance stands out, and that's Jeremy's. He is joined by IR80, an iconic rock band from Australia. They mix their biggest hit with Jeremy's alt-rock song, and it is perfection.

At the end of the show, we all come back out on stage as they show brief clips of our performances. I watch my segment in disbelief. As the credits roll, we all walk to the edge of the stage to shake hands with audience members. I find my family and give them a small wave. I can feel Raine watching me, and I do everything in my power not to look at him. What an amazing night.

Then it hits me; I'll miss this.

Chapter Forty-One – Raine

I watch Julia greet fans and I'm filled with pride and frustration. She performed extremely well, and other than Jeremy's performance, her segment is the best of the night. A few of the other contestants also have a good shot and really upped their game. I didn't have to submit my scores until the end of the show, so I walk off the stage to finish up.

Then I make the rounds greeting some of the artists and bands. I've worked with some of the country artists on song collaborations, but I'm meeting many of the big-name artists for the first time. I'm like a kid in a candy store meeting so many of my career influences. Other than watching Julia, the love of my life, perform, this is a highlight of the night.

After everyone has cleared the arena, I walk back out on the empty stage staring around the room. If I leave this, I'll miss it, no doubt. Just then Julia walks out, hesitating when she sees me. I stop the urge to run and scoop her up in my arms. She walks toward me but stops when we're a few feet apart.

"Pretty amazing night, huh?" she says quietly, taking a tiny step closer to me.

"Are you kidding?" I ask. "More than amazing. You were wonderful, by the way."

"Andy held it together for me."

"You held your own."

"What about Jeremy and IR80 ...wow."

As we continue to talk, the space between us gets smaller. We're like magnets, pulling toward one another until we're standing a foot apart.

"Enough of the small talk," I say. "How are you? Are they keeping you safe?"

"They are," she says, looking down, then she looks up with a smirk on those lips that keep drawing me in. "As I said, I can always run up to your room if I'm in danger."

"You'd have security in tow and the jig would be up," I say, smiling back at her.

Julia looks directly into my eyes. "Raine, I know our call didn't go well … it's not that I don't care or that I don't love you, it's just …" and then she pauses, giving me a chance to cut in.

"Jules, I meant every word I said. I want to marry you. There is no one else." As I say these words, I reach out and grab her hand, pulling her closer to me.

"Raine … someone may be watching."

But I lean in and rest my head against hers, just for a moment. I breathe her in before pulling away and dropping her hand. Our timing couldn't have been more perfect as several stagehands walk out of the wings. We step away from each other, and then Julia quickly walks away, out of my sight.

Chapter Forty-Two – Julia

My driver runs us through a burger joint. I need a normal experience after tonight's show. I order a salad but can't pass on the fries. As I'm pulling away, my phone rings.

"Well, how are you, little miss rock star?" Tracy says coolly. I can just picture her as she says this. "Andy Mitchell ... seriously? I am *so* pissed right now." Her frustration with me is obvious.

I respond back as if I have no idea what she's talking about, "Really ... and why is that?"

"Because you didn't tell me you were singing with one of the hottest male artists ever! I would have flown out in an instant."

"I'm sure you would have," I respond dryly. "I'll try to get his autograph for you."

"You'd better ... well, I guess I should tell you, you rocked," she says, trying to sound glib. "You did, I'll admit it."

"Was it enough for you to vote for me?" I say, teasing my good friend.

"I think I could put in a vote."

"How very generous of you ... I bet IR80 or The Blue Tones will get your real vote."

"They come close but I'm still leaning toward you and Mr. Gorgeous."

"Thank you, my friend."

"Everything else, okay? You sound tired."

"I couldn't stay away from Raine onstage after the show tonight."

"What? Didn't I train you better than that?"

"We were careful. But I do know one thing. I can't quit after tonight. I had too much fun out there."

"That's my girl! And you deserve to stay. Jeremy is good, and your friend Aubrey can sing her butt off, but you connect with people in a unique way. The crowd is always silent when you sing. It's beautiful to watch. So, what's up for you now, kings and queens flying in for the next show?"

I laugh and by the end of the conversation, I promise to get her an Andy Mitchell signed photo. It's the least I can do.

When I get to the hotel, I shower and climb into bed with the reality of the night hitting me. I'm going to continue competing, but I seriously have got to stay away from Raine. I can't make the situation worse.

Chapter Forty-Three – Raine

I board a plane first thing the next morning. Too much work is waiting for me back home in Nashville. I had an exhausting, restless night thinking about Julia, and how I'm juggling the show with my regular schedule. I again contemplate quitting this entire charade.

As I sit on the plane, all I can do is think, and my mind is racing with all that has happened over the last few weeks. I had the woman I love back, and now I don't. Pretty shitty. Then there's Julia's safety and the fact I can't do a damn thing about that. Likely it was a "pap" trying to get a shot, but what if it wasn't? Now Julia won't see me alone. I had to take a cold shower last night after seeing her briefly onstage because the ache was unbearable. I'm physically and mentally sure this show is not worth any of it.

I glance at my phone and the new picture of Julia and Trent having lunch at his house appears. They sure do look friendly. Damn! I've got to come up with some way to fix this whole mess or I'm going to lose the only thing that really matters, and that's Julia.

I'm about to send her a quick text when I notice an email from Trent, which is odd. Why would he be contacting me? We aren't friends.

I read Trent's message and I'm instantly filled with fear. "Raine, I know you're surprised to hear from me, but I need to get in touch with you. I was on the side of the stage last night and I watched you with Julia. I need to talk to you about this. It doesn't seem right to me."

I close Trent's message and turn off my phone, leaning back hard in my seat, my eyes tightly clenched. I'm stuck on a plane for several hours, and there is nothing I can do. I knew my brief meeting with Julia onstage was risky, and now it's biting us in the ass as I sit helplessly on a plane.

Chapter Forty-Four – Julia

Today is unusual and we have a much-needed day off. I wake up early and hit the hotel gym. I run for thirty minutes on the treadmill, and then spend another thirty on the stationary spin bike. Being that close to Raine last night has left me with a lot of pent-up frustration.

After unsuccessfully trying to work this whole mess out with exercise, I head to read and relax by the pool. Maybe I'll even get a massage? All I know is I need to chill out, do nothing, and not worry about a thing.

I walk into the pool area, but I'm one of the only contestants out in the sun. I lather on the sunscreen, lean into a chair, and put my ear buds in. I don't want anything to destroy my day of relaxation and pampering.

I'm almost relaxed when my phone buzzes. I pick it up and read a message from Trent. My mouth instantly goes dry. Great. Now this. My day of relaxation is over.

I quickly text Trent back, 'Can we meet someplace to talk about this? It's a long story and I want you to have all the facts before you make any decisions.'

As I head to the elevator and back to my room, my phone buzzes with another message from Trent, 'I'll meet you at your main hotel bar in an hour. It should be deserted this time of day, and we can speak privately.'

I have enough time to shower and change. I take a deep breath, trying to calm myself down as I walk into the bar area, looking for Trent. He's seated at a table with a drink in his hand.

"Right on time," Trent says as he stands to greet me.

I casually lean in and give him a hug. Even with the knowledge he carries and the threat that he may use it, I still consider him a friend.

"I didn't want to keep you waiting."

Trent gestures toward a chair, and I sit next to him. A server has made it to the table, and I order an iced tea.

"I'm sure my message surprised you?" Trent asks.

"It did. But I'm glad you sent me a message, so I can explain. I want you to have all the facts."

Trent looks at me and nods as I continue. I relay my history with Raine and that I had no idea he was going to be on the show, and how surprised we both were.

"I can tell you love him … and by the looks of it, he loves you too," Trent replies. "But my concern is if it's clouding his judgment. What if he's giving you better scores than the other contestants? My name is now tied to this show, specifically with you because we wrote and sang together. You have to understand why I'm concerned."

"I know Raine's fair, Trent. He won't give me a score I don't deserve. I've offered more than once to quit the show," I say, and then pause before continuing, "and he's also offered to quit. Although it will look bad, we aren't doing anything wrong. Believe me though, I'm struggling with it."

"Honestly, Julia … it may be jealousy that got me riled up at first. I believe you, and I do believe you deserve to be in the show, but I'm sure you can understand my concern. It won't look right to the producers and many people watching and participating."

"Maybe you're right, Trent, but I've loved this opportunity. A dream has come true, and I have the chance I never thought I would get. You must understand how hard it is to give it up, and truly, I had no idea Raine was a part of the show."

"As a former performer, I do understand, and I do believe you." Trent puts his drink down and continues, "I left a message for Raine, but I haven't heard back from him yet?"

"He had to fly to Nashville to take care of some business. I'm sure he'll call as soon as he's landed."

Just then, Trent's phone rings. He glances at the screen, nods toward me, gets up, and walks away from the table. My guess is he's asking Raine for his side of the story. After many minutes pass, he clicks off his phone and walks back toward me.

"I knew he'd give the same version. He offered to quit today to keep you on the show." Trent pauses, then continues looking directly at me, "Okay, I won't say anything, but if you get to the final four, you have to think hard about continuing. Eventually, people will find out about your relationship. It's inevitable. It's one thing if a relationship between you two started because of, or after the show, but you had a prior relationship. It's a conflict of interest. People won't like it and could destroy your career."

"You're right," I say, nodding in agreement.

We say our goodbyes and when I'm back in my room, I immediately call Raine.

I don't even say hello and my voice is hard and calm. "He won't say a word unless I make it to the final four, then we've got to think long and hard about the next steps."

"I may quit before then," Raine replies stoically.

"It would only raise questions about why." After I pause for a moment, my steely words just come out, "Raine, this relationship has never been easy between us and now it's ruining everything in my future. I want you to stay clear of me. Don't call me, don't text me, don't even acknowledge me at the show. You need to act like you've never met me, and I'll do the same."

With this, I hang up, not giving him a chance to respond. Tears are streaming down my face. Seeing Raine again was a mistake. Things never work out between us, and now look at what's happened? Raine Wagner is wrecking my life and my hopes, again.

Chapter Forty-Five – Raine

I've been back in Nashville for a day. It's early morning and I'm standing in my kitchen, trying to pull the freight train off my head with some strong coffee and half a bottle of Ibuprofen. Yesterday was a grueling day catching up with my real job here at home. When I add this to the stress of the show, flying back and forth, and now losing the love of my life, it's all taken its toll. The half-empty bottle of bourbon on my kitchen counter definitely didn't help.

When I got home last night, all I could do was stare at my empty king-sized bed and picture Julia. I finally gave up any possibility of sleeping in my bedroom, went outside on my patio, and somehow managed to drink the night away.

After a good couple of cups of coffee, I call Bret and tell him what happened with Trent and with Julia.

"Trent sounds fair and won't do anything rash," Bret says calmly, but I can tell he's pissed too.

"He won't, but who are we kidding? This is going to end badly."

"Maybe, maybe not. I have an idea. You'll need to come clean sooner rather than later, but you may be able to still save your career and get Julia back."

"What do you have in mind?"

Bret walks me through a couple of scenarios and what he thinks I could do. It involves completely putting myself out there, but I don't care; I'll do anything to clean up this mess. For the first time in many days, I think there may be a way out of this dilemma that won't obliterate our careers, and I may win Julia back in the process.

Chapter Forty-Six – Julia

I wake up the next morning, lying in bed and staring at the ceiling. I don't want to get up. Between crying all night and feeling sorry for myself, total and complete exhaustion has overwhelmed me. Too many people know about me and Raine or have photos and my reputation is about to be destroyed. I should just pack everything up and catch the next plane home.

But I can't. My family is arriving this morning, and because I have some time off before the next results show, we're supposed to sightsee around L.A. Great. I've got to act like I'm okay around a bunch of people who know me entirely too well. Unless our secret is exposed before the next results show, for now, I'm just going to take it a day, or even an hour, at a time.

Later that day, I gather my family up and we head out to Burbank for lunch. Almost everywhere we go, I end up surrounded by a small, but polite group of fans. I sign a few autographs and take some photos and although it interrupts our day, I'm reminded of how lucky I am. A few older women approach me, and I hear how they've been inspired to follow their own forgotten dreams. I notice my dad standing to the side, listening and looking so proud, which breaks my heart even more. My dad will be crushed when he hears the truth. I'll disappoint them all, especially him. I can barely look at him as we make our way back to the waiting car. I smile and pretend but Jody keeps looking at me questioningly. Jody knows something is up and she quietly pulls me aside at one point during the day.

"What's up, Jules? You seem distracted," she says with that same older sister look of concern I've seen for years.

"Well, I wanted to wait until the right moment, but I guess that moment is now ... you know I dated Raine back in Nashville?"

Jody nods. "Uh-huh," she says with hesitation.

"Well ... we ... um, we ... have become close during the show," I say, realizing this is much harder than I thought. Luckily, Jody jumps in.

"You've been seeing him again and now you're worried about how it will look?"

I'm a bit stunned but not really. Jody's a sharp cookie. "Yep, you nailed it, but it's not just that ... it seems like I have to make a choice about staying or leaving the show. You watched dad today, this would crush him ... I don't know what I should do or say? And then there's Raine. I've always been in love with him, but this all seems too hard and now all of it could ruin both of our careers. But if I leave the show, I'm not sure it will help. I don't know what to do?"

"You have to follow your heart, Jules. What would you give up everything for? There's your answer."

I look at her and give her a slight smile, nodding in agreement. I don't know if I have the exact answer to that yet. I love music, and today hearing the reaction from fans has been amazing, but Raine is the love of my life. It seems that no matter what I do, I'm going to lose and lose big.

The next day we're heading up to Santa Barbara. I've rented a large SUV, and we're going to drive along the coast to get away from the crowds. After talking with Jody yesterday and thinking about it all night, I've decided to let everyone know all that has happened.

As we drive along the coast, I tell everyone about my relationship with Raine, omitting certain details, of course. I tell them about Bethany, Trent, and that I'm thinking about quitting the show, so I can come out of this cleanly, letting the chips fall where they may. I don't tell them about Raine's proposal. I don't want to ugly cry.

When I finish, everyone is quiet until my dad finally speaks. "If Raine has scored you fairly, I don't think either of you have done anything wrong, but I'm glad you told us the truth before we read it somewhere. You do what you think you need to do for you."

I nod and smile. My dad's always right, and as we reach Santa Barbara and near the coast, I have to decide what is really in my heart. Greeting fans and hearing what they have to say has been incredibly powerful. I love music so much, and I love Raine, but it doesn't seem like the stars are aligning to allow me to have either one.

Later that night, I call Tracy. "Well, I told everyone the truth, so I'll make my decision after they announce the final eight."

Tracy is sympathetic and tries to be hopeful. "You know, you need to have more faith in the public. I don't think this is as bad as you think."

"It looks bad, Trace. There's no way around it. I've slept with a judge, and I should be disqualified. Doesn't matter if I deserve to be here, it's not right."

I end the call and the only thought playing in my mind is that I've got to figure out a way to salvage my reputation, without destroying Raine's career in the process.

Chapter Forty-Seven – Julia

I'm backstage with the other contestants watching pop sensation and our big performer of the night, Michael Reed, perform. As expected, he's absolutely amazing. With more than one hundred million records sold, the singer, songwriter, record producer, and actor has won too many awards to count. I'm totally starstruck.

Following a quick commercial break, the show plays clips of all of us. They show an old recording of me in high school during a school musical, with my mound of big hair and terrible makeup. The other contestants look toward me, and we all laugh.

After the clips, they seat our entire group on stage for the remainder of the show. Then the first group of four contestants joins Katy Reynolds center stage. Aubrey and Jeremy are in this first group, and both make it through. Two of the other female performers, both exceptional, are cut.

I sigh heavily as they go to break, hoping I won't have to wait until the end of the show to find out my outcome. I don't need any more pressure. After the break, they show segments of the judges during a typical day. Raine is in Nashville working with an artist in the studio, running around to pitch meetings and constantly on the phone. It's his typical day and it looks exhausting. My chest tightens as I watch him on the big screen. They show the same video clips for Brandi and Davis, and the reality of their hectic lives is not lost on me.

They bring up the next group of four, and thank God, I'm one of them. They announce the first saved contestant, and it's a young, cute male performer from Ohio, and all the girls in the audience scream. As they announce the next person who will stay out of the three, I hold my breath in the now silent room.

"And the next performer continuing on *Next Real Star* is … Julia Tate!"

The crowd erupts as I lean in to hug the other two performers who are going home. I didn't realize I was holding my breath, and I exhale with relief.

I wave to the crowd and catch Raine's eye. He's expressionless with his arms crossed in front of him. As I walk off the stage, I can feel his eyes following my every step.

Later that night, I'm with the other contestants attending a reception. The group includes Jeremy, Aubrey, and five other diverse talents. I think any one of them will be a great winner, as I'll soon be out of the competition.

I make the rounds and say hello to Trent, but I can barely meet his eyes. I try to physically avoid Raine, but whenever I walk around the room, I can feel him watching me. His face is still blank, and he doesn't smile at all.

Chapter Forty-Eight – Raine

Before tonight's show, I was wound up tight as never before as adrenaline seeped through every pore. All I wanted was for Julia to make it to the top eight and move on.

When they announced she was staying, I let out an enormous sigh of relief. I had prayed she'd move on, and deservedly so, but I wasn't sure. I'm so proud of her. Now I know what I have to do, and I can sit back and enjoy the rest of the show. Julia is one of the lucky remaining eight, and I smile knowing my plan will move forward.

At the end of the show, I run into Trent, who walks over to shake my hand as he gives me a knowing nod. I haven't said anything to him other than a text that I'll do the right thing when I need to.

##

The next morning, I'm headed out to meet Bret at the golf course and when I open my hotel room door, there's a manila envelope lying just outside the door frame. I figure it's from the show's producers, but the outside of the envelope is blank.

I cautiously open it up and walk over to sit on the edge of the bed, stunned at the contents. In the unmarked envelope are several pictures of me with Julia taken around Nashville, and even one at my house. Many of the shots show us embracing and even kissing. Although the photos were taken years ago, it looks like they are recent. There's only one person who could have been stalking me back then, and that's Bethany. I quietly place the photos into the envelope, and then I smile. This is exactly what I needed to help put my plan in motion. Bethany's little ploy will actually help me.

Chapter Forty-Nine – Julia

The next two days are a blur. As a part of the final eight, the pressure has escalated and we're all taking part in dozens of TV and radio interviews. After we finish taping, we head to the arena to tape a promo for the show's main sponsor.

I'm totally exhausted and haven't had any time to practice my next song. Luckily, I know it like the back of my hand, but it has to go off without a hitch. Later, I'm talking with Tracy about the show.

"Tomorrow night is it, right?" Tracy asks. "I really wish you'd change your mind about this."

"Nope. There are too many people digging up dirt. The sooner I'm out of here, the better. My family knows, so it won't be a big shock to them. It's the right thing to do, Trace."

"Well ... you know I think you should stay and tough it out. The fans are more forgiving than you may think. Have you talked to Raine about this? What does he think?"

"The fans may be forgiving, but I still need to make a clean break. And no, I haven't talked to Raine about this, so he doesn't know that I plan to leave after tomorrow's show. I told him to stay away and not contact me, and he's doing it." And the thought crosses my mind about how easily he dropped me, again, without a fight.

We end our call and I run through how it will all unfold at the show. I have to carefully think through each step of my performance. I'm going to sing as usual, but then when I'm done, I'll post that I've quit on social media, citing personal reasons, and head home. I've already bought a red-eye plane ticket, so it's less likely that any paparazzi will see me. This way, no one finds out about Raine, and I can sneak out of town. The posts are written and ready to go. All Tracy has to do is pull the trigger.

##

When I enter the green room later that day, the other remaining female contestants are already there. I join Aubrey and an artist in her mid-twenties, Monica. We're the only three women left in the competition.

Tonight, I'm wearing a simple sheath dress and boots, and I'll perform with just my guitar, singing a song I wrote more than fifteen years earlier. Although it's simple and written before I met Raine, I think it fits the situation.

As show time nears, I'm actually glad I'll sing last because now I can enjoy all of the other performances before me. While number seven performs, I make my way to the wing, knowing this is the last time I'll take the stage. I thought I'd be shaking or worse at this point, but instead I'm filled with a deep calm, knowing I'm doing the right thing.

##

When they announce my name, I walk out onto the stage waving to the crowd. I sit on a stool, and someone yells, "We love you, Julia!"

I smile and say softly into the microphone, "I love you, too." I take a mental picture to capture this moment.

The room quiets down as I begin to play my guitar. As I start to sing, I close my eyes and live and breathe each word. It's a song about surviving your first heartbreak and the helplessness you feel when you can't get that person out of your skin. After the bridge and before the last chorus, I'm suddenly jolted and instantly stop performing because Raine is standing right next to me. How he got up on stage, I've no clue. He's carrying a large, yellow envelope. I just sit there, staring at him in disbelief.

"Julia … wait …" Raine says, taking my microphone out of the stand. He turns and looks at the audience and continues, "There is something I need to tell all of you." He pauses for several seconds, but it feels like forever. I

147

continue to sit there stunned, staring wide-eyed at him.

"Many years ago, back in Nashville, I fell in love with someone, and next to music, she is the love of my life. That person is the woman next to me right now, Julia Tate."

I hear a few loud gasps but the majority of people in the room are in a shocked silence, and they look at one another stunned. From the side of the stage, I can see Katy and the show's producers all looking at each other, unsure of what they should do.

Raine continues, "For many reasons, our relationship never worked out back in Nashville, but we've reconnected because of this show. I'm telling you this because I don't want there to be any secrets between us." He pauses, takes a deep breath, and continues, "When I agreed to be a judge, I had no idea Julia was going to be a contestant on the show."

Raine pauses as he looks around at the audience, at me, and at everyone in the wings. "I know you're all surprised right now, but I want you to know that I have always graded Julia, and every contestant, fairly. Julia deserves to be exactly where she is right now. She hasn't done anything wrong. People have been trying to dig up dirt on us from many years ago, and in fact, I received an envelope today with pictures someone was trying to use against us, so I came up here tonight to tell you the truth."

Raine turns toward me as I sit there next to him, my mouth slightly agape. "Julia, you deserve to stay on this show. No one, not a photographer, or anyone trying to create a torrid story, should take this away from you."

Raine looks directly toward the camera. "I love Julia Tate more than I've ever loved anyone in my life." He turns and addresses the crowd, "She deserves to be here, and I hope everyone watching will give her the chance to continue."

Raine then puts the microphone back in the stand, pulls me up to a standing position, and lays a huge kiss on my lips in front of the audience and the millions of people watching. One of my hands is still holding my guitar, but the other wraps tightly around his waist as I kiss him back deeply.

Most of the audience is in a state of shock, but several people clap. When we finally draw apart, they immediately go to a commercial break. I look up at Raine, still stunned but smiling. He has a grin bigger than Texas as we embrace again in front of the crowd. At this point, I don't care. He took the blame and came forward. He stood up for me when I needed him the most, and I'm floored.

##

After the commercial break, Katy does her best to regain control of the show. They air segments of all eight performers while urging viewers to vote for the artist they want to move forward. When it comes to my segment, many people in the crowd cheer enthusiastically, but some audience members are still in shock.

When the cameras finally go dark, several producers run over to the side of the stage and grab me and Raine, steering us into a private room. I see several other contestants watch us in amazement.

After the door closes, the entire show staff surrounds us as the executive producer bellows, "Raine … what the? Really? What were you two thinking?"

"It's the truth," Raine replies. "Yes, we dated years ago, and we did reconnect during the show, but before the show started, I had no idea Julia was a contestant, and she had no idea I was a judge."

"Raine … this is a disaster. You'll probably have to leave the show," the producer replies. "As for you, Julia," he says turning to me as he speaks, "I'm not sure what we can do. I don't think you can stay."

Raine bellows back, "Release my scores. Let the entire world see how I judged Julia and all the other contestants, and you'll have no reason to doubt my integrity."

"We could, but what will the voters think? Really, it's up to them if they want to keep Julia. We'll see how everyone votes. I'll tell you one thing though. You two are blowing up on Twitter."

Chapter Fifty – Julia

I'm riding in my car with my family and it's so quiet, I can hear the tires as they rhythmically run along the street. Finally, Jody breaks the awkward silence.

"Well, he definitely loves you, that's for sure. That was one heck of a kiss."

A few seconds later, everyone is laughing, and soon I have tears running down my face. We all decide to order a celebratory dinner in one of the suites and make the most of this eventful night that likely destroyed my career and reputation. Shortly afterward we are enjoying our appetizers and champagne when Raine calls from his car.

"Hey … I just arrived at the hotel, can I come up?" he asks hesitantly.

I'm in a lighthearted mood all things considered. "We're all up in suite 1418, we've got champagne and dinner will arrive soon. We'll celebrate the fact that you got fired, and I'm going to be voted off the show."

"I'm on my way."

When Raine enters the room, a good-hearted cheer erupts from everyone. I walk toward him and as he sheepishly looks at me, I jump into his arms and he kisses me on the cheek. Jody walks up and gives him a quick hug, then he makes the rounds greeting everyone. I watch in silence when he reaches my dad. Raine shakes his hand and leans in, whispering in my dad's ear. A few seconds later, they both step out into the hallway. Jody looks at me questioningly, but I shrug my shoulders, taking a sip of champagne as I look away.

A few minutes later, when Raine and my dad walk back in the room, my dad is grinning from ear to ear. I look at Raine and he gives me a huge smile.

My heart stops for a moment. It's done. Raine spoke with my father.

My dad grabs a glass of champagne and raises it in the air as he speaks, "To Julia and my soon to be new son-in-law." Everyone cheers.

I walk to Raine as he enfolds me in his arms. We no longer have to hide and it's official. We're engaged.

After our fun-filled family dinner, Raine takes my hand in his and it sends shivers up my arm as he leads me toward the door. There are catcalls behind us, but I don't care. We're headed to my room, no longer afraid of who sees us or takes our picture. As we wait for the elevator doors to open, Raine pulls me in front of him, my back to his chest as he runs his lips along the back of my neck, his hands tightly gripping my waist. He hears my intake of breath, and chuckles deep in his throat.

"Don't you think we need to wait a few minutes?" I ask with a light laugh, just as the elevator doors open, and an older couple walks out. They're not amused. Raine grabs me and pushes me inside the elevator as his lips work their way to mine.

"I don't care ..."

He whips me around again with my back pressed against his chest as I struggle to push the button so the door will close. Again, he is running his lips along the back of my neck, which sends a tingle down my spine and to all the right places. He has me pulled hard against him with one hand running up my thigh as the other hand is groping my right breast.

"Raine!" I say laughing. "I'm sure there are cameras!"

Again, he replies, his lips lightly kissing my neck and down my jawline, "I don't care."

I laugh as I reach my hands around and grab his ass, pulling him hard against my backside. I can tell he's ready as he groans in frustration.

I laugh and say, "You started this."

And by now, thankfully, we've reached my floor. We only had to go down a few floors to my room, but it was one of the longest elevator rides of my life. As we step out, our arms entwined, Raine continues to tease me with his lips and hands. A security guard greets us asking to see my room key, but he's laughing and gives Raine a wink. I'm sure my face went fifty shades of red. I maneuver us in the door, which is not easy with Raine as my constant distraction, his hands all over me. When we're inside, Raine walks directly to the room's safe.

"What's the combination to this thing?"

"Not very original, my birth date," I say, collapsing on the bed, removing my shoes as I do. I won't need them.

Raine opens the safe and grabs the engagement ring. He pulls the ring out of the box and walks toward me, stops, and kneels. "After this show bullshit was over, we said we'd make it official," he says, a huge grin filling his face.

"Wait a minute, did you just propose? Was that a proposal?" I tease.

"Good lord, woman, after the last few hours, really? You ask me that?"

I laugh, my hand going to my mouth as he places the ring on my finger, and then he pulls my face toward his.

"Your dad said he approves, so now you are all mine. And I think now you'll have plenty of time on your hands to plan an October wedding."

My face falls as I remember I'm likely cut from the show and my career is destroyed.

"Hon … I didn't mean it like that," he says softly. "You're a talented writer, and maybe the voters will give you a chance. If not during this competition, just let the controversy die down … you'll see."

I look at him as tears form on my eyes, "I know you're right and I am so happy right now. Happier than I have ever been, truly." A few seconds pass as I realize the one thing I thought I was fighting for doesn't compare to my love for Raine. "Screw my career. If I have you, I've won."

Raine kisses me deeply. We have many free hours tonight and we're not going to waste a minute.

I quickly strip down, removing every ounce of clothing as Raine does the same, our eyes locked the entire time. He grabs me with abandon and picks me up as I wrap my legs around him. He walks to the bed and sits with my legs around him and we join quickly.

Raine isn't soft and sweet. He's filled with latent, pent-up stress and energy. He's on fire and his hands are everywhere, moving from my body to my face, his touch hot on my skin. We fall to the floor.

In kind, I let myself go like I haven't in some time. I'm not concerned about who hears or what anyone thinks as I cry out with each of his thrusts. All I want to do is bring him pleasure. I'm forceful, demanding, and urgent. In less than ten minutes, we're both spent, gasping on the floor.

Raine gathers me in his arms so tightly, I almost can't breathe.

"Well, that was interesting ... and amazing," he says, still catching his breath, his lips grazing the side of my neck.

"Worked for me," I say jokingly. "Or couldn't you tell?"

"Oh ... I could tell. Every time ... I could tell," he says, smirking.

I laugh and reply, "We need to work on that. I expect much more from you in the future."

"Your wish is my command." Then Raine picks me up, carries me to the bed, and we start again.

Chapter Fifty-One – Julia

The next morning, for the first time, I walk out of the hotel with Raine by my side. As we head to my waiting car, a swarm of reporters and photographers surround us. Luckily, security helps us get into the car. We both smile for the cameras but to the many questions yelled our way, I reply, "No comment."

The show's producers called me first thing that morning, and we're on the way to meet with them. This can't be good news, but as I look over at Raine's profile, I don't care. Now we can begin our life together back in Nashville.

As we walk in and greet the show's staff, Raine clutches my hand and gives it a tight squeeze. The producers ask if they can speak with me privately, and I follow them into one of the large green rooms.

The head producer cuts right to the chase. "Julia, you must know how shocked we all were last night during your performance and Raine's announcement?"

I quickly reply, "Of course I do, and believe me, I never wanted this to happen."

"Well, the announcement definitely created buzz for the show and some in the network are calling for our jobs, but the president of the network ... well, he thinks the opposite."

"What do you mean?" I ask.

"The computer system crashed last night because we had so many votes come in, and the phones are off the hook. Most viewers are demanding we allow you to stay in the competition. The consensus seems to be that voters are glad the truth came out, and that Raine was the one who did it."

"Wow ... that's not what I thought I'd hear today."

"But the network president wants Raine off the show. He believes you both, and it's not that he doesn't like Raine, but as a judge, it just isn't right. We're also going to release his scores to all the contestants. We're not sure about releasing them to the public just yet."

"That's fine with me. Raine said he'd be happy to release them, but I don't agree that he has to leave the show."

"The only way you can stay is if Raine leaves."

"Shouldn't we bring him in on this discussion?"

"Julia, we want you to see his scores first."

"I know he was fair. I'd bet my life on it."

And he was fair, but I'm more than crushed to see Raine never scored me at the top. Not once. Raine's best scores went to Jeremy. After I review the scores, the producers ask Raine to join us. My stomach is now in knots, and I can hardly look Raine in the eyes when he comes back into the room. His first reaction to my very first live performance portrayed the truth about what he really thinks about my talent.

They tell Raine everything I just heard, including the fact that I just read his scores. Raine's head quickly swivels my way, and I look up at him and give him a slight, somewhat fake smile.

"Julia, I never thought you were any less of a performer than anyone else on the show, but my scores reflect the best performance, song, and marketability," Raine says while trying to look me directly in the eyes. "You are incredibly talented."

I continue to smile at him, but it doesn't reach my eyes as I reply, "Of course. I understand, Raine. It's business and you were doing your job."

The lead producer chimes in, "As we said, Raine, we can't let you continue with the show. We'll get some bad press keeping Julia, but it's a whole other issue keeping you as well."

"That's okay. She is all I care about," Raine says as he walks toward me and puts his arm around my shoulders. I loosely put my arm around his waist, but I won't look up at him.

Chapter Fifty-Two – Julia

Later that morning, I'm on the phone with Tracy. "Not once did he give me the best score. Can you believe it? Ouch."

"Julia, you're an amazing singer and it's one judge's scores," she says, trying to lift my spirits, but it's not helping. I sigh back loudly as she continues, "Obviously, you're doing well with the fans, and you get to stay on the show. Isn't that what's important?"

"I guess. But clearly, he doesn't like what I'm doing. Will he ever take what I do seriously? That was part of our issue before."

"You'll have to ask him about it."

We end the call and I have the rest of the day to take in all that's happened. All I want to do is get a relaxing massage and try to forget about everyone and everything, for once.

Raine has sent me several texts, but so far, I'm ignoring them. He finally calls.

"I almost sent a search party to look for you," he says, his tone clearly relaying his frustration.

"I'm okay, just trying to relax," I reply dryly. I'm sure he notices.

"Julia, we need to talk. I need to explain..."

But I cut him off. "There's nothing to explain. I know you were fair, and I can't fault you for that. It is what it is."

His tone becomes a bit fierce. "Let me come to your room."

"I'm going to get a massage, and then I'm having lunch with Aubrey. Let's meet later tonight." He gives in as long as I agree to dinner later in his room.

##

Following my semi-relaxing massage, Aubrey meets me at one of the hotel restaurants. A few photographers and fans follow me the entire way to the restaurant, and I smile and casually wave. They are kind about it, but I'm not in the mood for it today.

I greet Aubrey warmly as she approaches the table. She blurts out, "Jeez … I could barely make my way in here. Is this what it is like for you and Raine now?"

"Slightly worse actually."

Aubrey looks at me sympathetically, or maybe it's more like with embarrassment. "I read Raine's scores today. Julia, you have nothing to be disappointed about. Clearly, he liked Jeremy's performances. He had me scored low sometimes," she says jokingly. "How do you think that makes me feel?"

I give her a half-hearted smile. "But he's the person whose opinion matters most. I thought he'd give me the best score one night, but not even once."

"What can I say? Men suck."

I laugh, my spirits lifting. "No kidding. Let's eat, I'm starving."

We continue to talk about the next show, and we don't mention Raine's scores again.

Chapter Fifty-Three – Raine

I'm sitting at the hotel bar, on the phone with Bret. "Damn it, Bret, they gave Julia my scores and I didn't know they were going to. I needed to prep her first and tell her why I scored her the way I did. Now she's crushed. It's written all over her face. Jeremy was my first-place score."

Bret replies, "Well, you were honest, and this definitely will eliminate any doubt about your integrity."

"But I hurt her."

"That's a part of the game, man. Now you've got to say you're sorry. Comes with the territory. Julia's a cool chick, she'll understand."

I'm not so sure. The look on her face told me everything. She's devastated by my scores.

##

Later that night, I'm putting the finishing touches on the room trying to make sure everything is perfect. I have a nice bottle of Chardonnay, her favorite purple tulips, and dinner is on standby. I'll take care of her tonight. It's my last chance as I'm leaving for Nashville tomorrow. Since I'm no longer a judge, and I have so much work back home, it makes sense for me to go home. My big TV reveal and newfound celebrity have boosted my exposure. Many acts, including famous rock acts, are clamoring to work with me. Plus, I don't want to distract my girl.

But tonight, there is one person I've got to win back, and I will do everything in my power to make it up to her. Although I stand by my scores, the last thing I wanted to do was hurt Julia.

Chapter Fifty-Four – Julia

I've changed into jeans and a loose-fitting top. Although I'm happy I get to spend the night with Raine, the weight of his rejection still hangs on me.

I knock on his door, and it takes a few moments for him to respond. When he opens the door, I catch my breath. He's wearing black jeans, a form-fitting button-up shirt, and his cowboy boots. Be still, my heart. Next to seeing him in a suit and tie, this is the look I like best. I walk in and instantly notice the flowers. They're everywhere.

"Oh Raine, my favorite," I say, walking over toward a bouquet. "They're beautiful."

"Not as beautiful as you," he says, walking over and wrapping his arms around me, but I'm stiff and pull away. I go to the edge of a couch and sit down.

Raine says nervously, "I'll order dinner soon, but first, I have something for you."

My eyes follow him as he walks to his safe and pulls out a small Tiffany's box. I protest, "I don't need more jewelry, hon. The ring is plenty."

"Who said this was for you?" he says with a smirk, looking down at me with the Tiffany's box in his outstretched hands.

I give him a sly, questioning look. "You're giving me something not meant for me?"

"Just open the dang box," Raine says laughing. Then he sits down next to me and watches me unwrap the smaller, rectangular box covered in blue paper.

I open it and gasp out loud, my hand coming up to my mouth. I look at him and smile as tears form, which will totally mess up my mascara-covered lashes. As I pull a tiny silver rattle from the box, Raine's own eyes are filled with tears. I turn and fall into his warm, strong arms.

"Raine … it's beautiful. But why this … and why now?"

"You remember the last time we were together?"

I look at him and blush slightly, my hand unconsciously going up to my face, "How could I forget?"

"Exactly. Do you realize we made love without using a condom? What if we got lucky? I'm just being proactive."

My head goes back, and I laugh out loud. "I love it. I absolutely love it."

His simple, yet amazingly thoughtful gesture brings me back to what is really important. That I'm here right now with the man I love more than anything. I decide to let him off the hook about the scores.

"About your scores," I say, looking up at him with all seriousness. "I know why you were leaning toward Jeremy. He's incredibly talented and it will be tough for anyone to beat him. I just want you to take me seriously after this. My career is just as important as yours."

"Are you kidding? Of course your career is as important as mine … maybe more so." Raine stops and takes my face in his hands as he continues, "You are the most amazing, talented woman I've ever known." Then he kisses me deeply and pulls his face back and smiles, his green eyes softly looking directly into mine. Following a delightful dinner, Raine keeps me preoccupied and I forget all about his stupid scores.

##

I spend the next few days relaxing at the hotel. I don't have a choice. Everywhere I go I'm stopped for pictures and autographs. I can't really leave and coupled with the pressure of the last few days, it's starting to take a toll.

We're waiting to hear who will replace Raine as a new judge. Many celebrities want Raine's spot, and I anxiously wonder who will replace him, but as usual, we won't find out until show time. Tracy has flown in for this next show and we're sitting out on my balcony, drinking coffee.

Tracy casually mentions, "Another trash magazine had pictures of you and

Raine at the airport. They just can't get enough."

"Yep, I was there," I joke. "I do think all of this will die down soon. At least, I hope so. Good lord."

"Any idea on the new judge?"

"Not really. A couple of female country icons are being tossed around, and Trent's name has come up, but I hope it's not him. Controversy there too."

"Have you talked to Raine today? How's he doing back in Nashville with you here?"

"We're coping," I say, giving her a knowing smile. "He sent me a text first thing this morning. He's crazy busy with regular work and a couple of national interviews about the show."

"At least you're public now, a big load off of your shoulders."

"Definitely ... but boy, do I miss him. It's painful."

"Is he coming to the show tonight?"

"We both thought it would be best if he stays away. There's a good chance I'll be cut anyway. Who knows how everyone will vote."

"Whatever happens, what a ride this has been."

"You got that right, sister. What a glorious ride."

Chapter Fifty-Five – Raine

I've just gotten off the phone with a florist. If I can't be there in person, I want Julia to have a daily reminder. If she's lucky enough to make the final four, she'll have fresh flowers every day we're apart.

Because of how the last show went down, they aren't using any of the judges' scores. The voting public will decide who stays and who goes.

My phone rings; it's Bret. "Our writing appointment is at two, right?" Bret asks. "You're so busy now, I need to make sure I get my time in with the hottest producer in Nashville," he says, obvious sarcasm oozing through the phone.

"Funny. I would never miss our appointment. I'll tell you what though, I need an assistant to help me deal with everything. I can't keep up," I say as I pace around my kitchen, running my hand down my unshaven face.

"Controversy sells records."

"What?" I ask, pausing to lean wearily against my counter.

"Your torrid love affair has made you one of the most sought-after producers in the world. Controversy gets everyone talking."

"But it's talent that keeps them wanting to work with you."

"How do you think your girl's gonna do tonight?"

"Not sure, and I'm a fucking wreck." This is an understatement. The pacing I've been doing has been constant. I continue, "I have no idea how this is going to go for her … I just don't want to see her crushed if this doesn't go her way."

"Well, at least we'll get a good song out of this."

Chapter Fifty-Six – Julia

As show time nears, I can hardly keep still. After my call with Tracy, I went to the gym for hours and then took a hot bath, but nothing is working. I'll likely end up humiliated in front of everyone on national television. My phone has been buzzing all day and I've been ignoring it until I get a call from Raine.

"Hey babe," I say sweetly. "The flowers are beautiful. Absolutely beautiful."

"My way to make sure you don't forget about me."

"Highly unlikely."

Raine must hear the tension in my voice. "No matter what happens, if you stay, or if you get to come home to me sooner, remember that I love you more than life. You're the most beautiful, smart, and talented woman I've ever known, and I want to make sure you heard me say talented. I mean that."

Instantly, the tension starts to ease out of my body, "I did hear it, and thank you for saying it."

"Of course. And just remember, some of the people who didn't win have bigger careers than the actual winners. No matter what, I know you'll move on to bigger and better things."

"I hope so," I say before teasing him, "Do you think I could even get a hot-shot producer like you to work with me?"

"I don't know. I'm pretty expensive now," he says sarcastically. "But I think I could work something out with you though."

"A trade agreement?"

"Something like that."

And I laugh out loud.

##

Later that day when I enter the arena, to say the place is buzzing is an understatement. Everyone is running around like their hair is on fire. They've moved our final eight into one large room with dividers to separate out the men and women, but everyone can watch the big screen together. I'm glad they finally moved us all into one room.

"Are you as nervous as I am?" Aubrey asks as she touches up her makeup.

"Pretty sure I'm more nervous than you."

"Understandable. Whatever happens, I'm glad to have met you, and I hope we stay friends outside of this show."

"Of course," I say, leaning in to give her a hug. "I wouldn't have it any other way."

Again tonight, they'll have guest performers around each contestant's announcement until we are down to the final four. As we all surround the large TV screen, I anxiously wait to see who will replace Raine.

As the lights come up, Katy Reynolds takes center stage. "Many of you watched the drama unfold last week, but in case you didn't, here's what you missed."

Clips of seven of the other contestants performing come on in sequence, and then finally my performance comes on, complete with Raine's interruption. My heart is in my throat watching Raine on the screen. I've never watched any of this footage, and my face is now flaming red. Several performers, including Jeremy, give me sympathetic smiles. Then it's time for us to gather on stage. They'll announce the final eight one by one, and of course, I'm last. The drama.

Katy comes on the screen and says, "After much consideration, and the fact that a new judge will only have to provide scores for one more show, we've decided to eliminate the third judge position. Brandi and Davis's scores combined with viewers' votes will determine the scores for our final show. Now, let's bring out your final eight … after a word from our sponsor," and the crowd groans.

As we make our way to the stage, you could wring out my hands. When we're live, they call each of us out individually. As I step to the edge of the stage to follow Jeremy, I have no idea how the crowd will react.

As Katy says my name, my legs feel like they are cemented to the floor. I don't want to leave the side of the stage. I step out and wait for the "boos" but all I hear are cheers and applause. Almost as loud as Jeremy's. Inside, I'm floored. I walk to center stage and join hands with the other contestants. We've become a tight group, and it will be hard to cut our number in half.

They move us to the side of the stage. Katy announces the first performer of the night, and everyone is surprised when judge Brandi Singleton and her dancers take the stage to perform one of her biggest hits.

I look out at the screaming crowd and then back to Brandi, who still has it. She's an amazing performer. After the next commercial break, we're back live and the first person to leave will be announced.

Katy calls Aubrey center stage. "And after tallying the votes, Aubrey Wilson, you'll be …" a long pause … "Aubrey, you'll be leaving *Next Real Star.*"

Many in the crowd boo as Aubrey, obviously disappointed, turns and watches her show highlight reel. I can barely hold back my tears.

Chapter Fifty-Seven – Raine

Bret is sitting with me in my living room, watching the show unfold. I stand to cheer and clap loudly in front of the TV when Julia walks on the stage.

"I think she actually heard you all the way in L.A.," Bret says, rubbing his ear.

"I want her to hear me in L.A., damn it. I can't believe I'm here and not there supporting her in person. This sucks."

Bret takes a long swig of his beer, before asking, "Are you going to be like this all night?"

I ignore him. "I'll tell you one thing, they had better keep Julia in this show. She deserves it."

Bret looks up toward the heavens, and I scowl at him. I drop on the couch, and we watch Brandi perform. After it's announced that Aubrey will leave, my anxiety grows.

"One woman down and only two left. This is why Jeremy will win. Women almost never win these shows."

"I beg your pardon. What about Jerrie Simpson and Pamela Watson?" Bret says, reminding me about two of the biggest female country recording artists of all time. I think Julia has a shot, contrary to your scores, my friend," Bret says jokingly as he gets up to grab another beer. "You need another?"

"If you bring up my scores again, I'll have to switch to something stronger," I say, glaring at my friend. He sure can push my buttons.

"Got it ... one bourbon coming up."

The cameras pan to the remaining seven contestants before taking a commercial break. Julia looks nervous. Beautiful, but nervous.

After the next break, they call up Dewayne, a young R&B artist. He stays, and the crowd erupts. He's another favorite with the young girls.

Dewayne jumps up and down, hugs Katy, and then waves to the crowd as he makes his way offstage.

The next guest performer takes the stage, and then Jeremy is called up and easily goes through, leaving only two spots. They cut two more: a male pop vocalist, Steven Myer, and the other female contestant, Monica, is also eliminated. That leaves Rylie Cooper, a young country singer from Texas; Peter Robinson, an eclectic alt-rock singer and stellar guitar player; and Julia.

They move the remaining three to center stage, and after many tense moments it's announced that Peter will continue as the third contestant. This leaves Julia and Rylie, and only one will stay.

"I can't watch another minute of this," I fume. I'm now pacing in front of the TV.

"I feel like I'm watching a tennis match with you crossing like that," Bret says dryly. "Sit down. You're making me dizzy."

"She had better make it to the final four. Oh my God, I'm gonna be sick."

I walk to a leather chair and throw myself down heavily. The two-minute commercial break takes years off my life.

When they come out of break, Katy brings Julia and Rylie to center stage.

"And now we are down to the very last two. Rylie … Julia, how do you both feel right now?" Katy asks as she shoves the microphone in front of Rylie.

"Whatever happens, I'm glad to have made it this far," Rylie answers. Several girls scream.

Julia follows with, "I've said it all along, I won the first day I took the stage and performed. No matter what, I'm happy."

"Well, let's get down to it." Katy picks up her card and starts reading. "And the next, and final contestant moving on to the final four of *Next Real Star* is?" Katy pauses for several moments as people yell out their choice. Julia smiles at the crowd and then looks down. I'm holding my breath.

Katy finally says, "Julia Tate!"

I fall to my knees, my head resting on the floor.

"Dude, what in the hell are you doing, praying?" Bret teases.

"I think I just passed out. Thank God … I should be praying though."

We both watch as Julia smiles and takes her place with the other three remaining contestants. She made it to the final four.

Chapter Fifty-Eight – Julia

The four contestants who are leaving are packing up their stuff, and I walk over to Aubrey. Although this is one of the happiest nights of my life, I'm devastated to see my friend go.

"You have to carry on as the only female contestant left," Aubrey says. Her eyes are red from crying, and her makeup is pretty smudged up.

My eyes tear up as I lean in to give her a hug. "You bet, every move is for us. Dang it, girl, I don't know what I'll do without you here. It just won't be the same." I lean back and wipe under my eyes, trying to keep my mascara from running.

I give Aubrey another hug and then watch her walk out the door. She turns one last time and gives me a slight wave. My phone, which is sitting on a dressing room table in front of me, has been buzzing nonstop. I instantly go to a text from Raine.

'I almost had a heart attack (kidding). If Bret hadn't been sitting with me, I never would have made it through the show. Seriously though … YES!'

I reply, 'I know, YES! I literally can't believe this! I'm glad – surprised - relieved. Did I mention how much I miss you?'

A few seconds later he sends a message back, 'I'm sorry … I miss you, too. Just a little excited.'

And I smile to myself as I walk out the door to my waiting car.

Chapter Fifty-Nine – Julia and Raine

The next morning, I call Raine first thing. "I have an idea," I say groggily.

"Hey, babe. Spill it."

"On Thursday, I want you to perform a song we write together on the show. Win or lose, I want you on stage with me." I pause as I wait for his response. It's risky and I'm not entirely sure he'll agree, mainly because it could very well hurt my chances of winning.

Raine doesn't even hesitate. "You know I'd do anything to be by your side. That gives us two days to write a new song … or do you have something you're working on?"

"I've got a start, but I need you to help me finish it."

"I'll catch the next flight."

I hang up and smile, staring up at the ceiling and burying myself deeper under the covers. I barely slept picturing the two of us together on stage for my final song. I know it may sway some to vote against me. In fact, I'm sure it's not allowed, but I don't care. I want Raine by my side, and performing a song together seems like the perfect way to end the wild ride we've been on.

Finally, I drag myself out of bed. Just a few days remain, and if I win, it could change my life forever. But deep down I know I have all that really matters. I have Raine, and I don't need anything else.

##

I catch an afternoon flight and try to secretly make my way to Julia's hotel. I'm wearing a ball cap and glasses, but it doesn't help. Several people recognize me, and most are pleasant, although I did get a couple of mean looks. I chuckle to myself. One girl yells to me, "Tell Julia we're voting for her!" I smile and wave at the young fan as I race inside the hotel.

##

It's now Tuesday afternoon and I'm with the remaining contestants as we practice a group song we'll perform together. The song is a unique take on an old seventies rock song which Dewayne has mixed with a rap, giving it a funky, pop vibe.

It's late evening before we finally finish going over the show with the producers. I'll sing a ballad with my guitar and the entire house band but haven't given anyone any more details. I really have no idea what we'll come up with by show time, but Raine is a fantastic writer, so I'm not worried. All day, knowing I get to see him has me floating on air.

When I open my hotel room door, I can hear the shower running and Raine's suitcases are on the floor. I set my things down and strip off my clothes to join him.

I enter as silently as possible. Raine is singing and as I open the door, I startle him. He quickly grabs me, pulling me hard against him and under the hot water, kissing me on the lips as he runs his soapy hands all over my ass. I groan as he reaches around and puts his warm hand between my legs, firmly caressing.

"Damn, always feels like the first time," I say against his lips.

"Uh huh." And that's all he says as his lips make a trail to where his hand had just been and I gasp out loud as he kneels before me, my hands grasping his wet hair. A long, lingering shower ensues.

After we finish our delightful shower, I wrap myself up in a robe and I'm sitting on the bed with my guitar in my lap. Raine is facing me, and I'm showing him the chords and some of the melody I've started on.

Raine is watching my hands and says, "I like the chords and melody. Any ideas on lyrics?"

"None. I think I know the feel of where we need to go, but I want you to help me find the right words."

He stands and picks up his phone. "Play through it again, and I'll record it

171

for later. Since you've already created the basic structure, let me take a crack at the lyrics."

I smile and nod. We finish the structure and chords of the song, and by the time we finish, it's late.

"Babe, you're exhausted," Raine says as he puts his guitar down and kneels in front of me. "Why don't you get some sleep and I'll work on lyrics? You need to be fresh tomorrow."

Many years ago, he rarely even noticed or cared that I was tired. Now, he's doing his best to take care of me. Talk about a one-eighty. I nod and hand him my guitar as he pulls the covers up around me and leans in to kiss me softly. My breath catches. Damn, he always smells amazing. I put my head down on the pillow and that's all I remember.

##

I walk to the bed and put my hand on Julia's head, running it softly over her hair. I've never been this content in my life. I pick up my phone and notepad, and walk out on the balcony, taking in the L.A. scenery. I put my earbuds in, hit play, and put down all the words that Julia makes me feel.

The sun is starting to rise when I finish. I think we've got a really good song. I walk back inside, put my stuff down, and run my hands over my now gruff face. I quietly undress, walk over, and pull the covers down next to her and climb into bed. I'm doing my best not to wake her, but she stirs and instantly nestles against me.

I pull her to me and stroke her hair as she half opens her eyes.

"I was having the most amazing dream," she says softly.

"Tell me."

"We were sitting on a porch watching children play in our huge yard. The sun was setting. It was absolutely gorgeous."

She leans up and puts her lips on mine. "I want to make it a reality... right now."

Julia presses against me clear in her intentions as I chuckle deep in my throat, pulling her underneath me. She fell asleep in her robe, and I easily maneuver between her legs. She welcomes me to her. Although exhausted,

I'm instantly renewed and rise on my forearms. I watch her face as I slowly bury myself inside of her. She raises her hips to greet me, her eyes still half shut, and she moans softly. We make slow, silent love. I can't get enough of this woman or her body. I gently carry her to release several times before we come together as one, her arms gripping me tightly. I fall asleep spent, holding her tight against my body. It's a perfect ending to a productive night.

Chapter Sixty – Raine and Julia

My eyes open and I roll over, instantly noticing Julia's not in bed with me. I push myself up to a sitting position and find her on the couch, reading my lyrics.

"What do you think?" I manage to croak out, the lack of sleep taking its toll.

"Wow ... I had no idea. I know how much I love you, but this," she pauses. "This is incredible."

"I just put down what we mean to one another."

"This is perfect."

The sun is well up. Julia let me get some much-needed sleep. "What time is it? Don't you have to go to the arena today?" I say, concerned.

"It's only about nine and you've only been asleep for a few hours. Don't worry. I don't have to be at the arena until later this afternoon."

"Then I think you need to get your butt back in bed with me this instant."

Julia laughs and quickly climbs off the couch, giving me a slight salute. She jumps into bed with me, resting her head against my chest. I play with her hair, neither of us saying a word as we both drift back to sleep.

##

They've reserved the arena for me to rehearse with the band. I only have an hour to show them the song and work up what I want to do. We found out earlier that each of us will get a guest producer, and when country icon and actress Reilley Jane walks through the door, I literally almost faint.

"Oh ... my ... word!" I exclaim, hardly containing myself. "This is like winning the lottery. I cannot believe this."

Reilley just smiles, walks over to me, and gives me a big hug like we're long-lost friends. "What do you say we make sure you win this thing?" Reilley drawls, her eyes twinkling. "You're representing all the women out there right now who deserve this chance."

Raine has charted the music for the band members, and I hand a copy of the lyrics to Reilley, giving her a few minutes to look them over.

"Wow, did you write this?" Reilley asks.

"Raine actually wrote most of the lyrics," I reply.

"It's amazing."

We spend the next hour hammering out the details and dynamics of the song, but I never let on that Raine is going to join me onstage to sing.

When we're done, I have a few interviews to finish with the others. We're taping a radio interview and prepping for a streamed morning TV show appearance we'll do at 5 a.m. sharp tomorrow.

I'm heading out to my car when a young man approaches. Although I've got security with me, the man gets close enough to throw something at me.

"Slut ... you don't deserve to win," he yells as security grabs him and pulls him away. They quickly get me into my car, and we speed off.

I push myself back against the backseat, the shock still registering.

"Are you okay?" the driver asks, looking at me through the rear view.

I just nod. I pick up my phone and almost call Raine but decide against it. I have to think this through. His overprotective nature will come roaring out. That is a given.

I send Raine a quick text asking him to meet me at one of the hotel bars. You need a key to get into this area, and I hope it will be quiet. I stare out of the car window as we speed toward the lobby entrance.

I instantly know something is wrong, but Julia isn't talking. She's been so quiet, and I just keep asking her what's wrong but she's not really saying anything. She's about to finish her second glass of wine when I again push her to tell me something. "What happened? Did the rehearsal go okay?"

"Yeah, it was great," she says. "I told you about Reilley, right?"

I nod. This is the only piece of information I've been able to get out of her. "What is it? Please, tell me."

Julia lowers her head and then slowly raises her eyes to mine. "As I was walking toward my car today after rehearsal, a guy approached, and then yelled something as he threw a liquid of some kind at me ... but it didn't get on me, he was too far away." The words tumble out of her mouth. My blood is boiling with each of her words.

"What! Are you kidding me?" I instantly stand, looking around the room. "Where was security? That's ridiculous!"

"Security came and got him right away. It happened so fast I didn't have time to react."

"He yelled something? What did he say?" I ask, my words dripping with a cool fierceness of protection.

"I think he called me a slut."

"A slut," I say as I run my hand through my hair and down my face. "Son-of-a ... you're never going to that arena again without me. I can't believe this!" I'm now pacing around her at the table, on guard.

"He wasn't exactly off target, Raine. I'm unmarried and sleeping with one of the show's former judges. Technically, he may be right," Julia says with a slight grin, clearly trying to shake my current mood, but it doesn't work.

"*No* ... you're not a slut, and tomorrow you're wearing your engagement ring. I want the entire world to know. We're telling everyone we're getting married in October."

Julia gives me a sly grin. "You know, you are kind of cute when you get all He-Man on me."

I drop back into my chair next to her. "You haven't seen anything yet," I say as I bend my head down, kissing her hard on the lips.

##

I wake up the next morning wrapped up in sheets with Raine's arm slung across my midsection. After yesterday's incident, Raine had insisted on escorting me to the room and wouldn't leave my side. Not that I minded.

He even called security and demanded an extra team outside my door.

Last night before bed, we had practiced our new song. Tonight will be the biggest of my career. We crashed hard after practice, but I woke up once and I'm now convinced Raine is trying to get me pregnant. Great. Pregnant and unwed, just the picture I want to portray to the world.

I sit up in bed and stretch my back, noticing the tension. It's still dark. We have an early call for our TV show appearance. Having Raine at tonight's show won't be a problem. He's already invited but getting him on the stage with me will be the hard part.

Raine stirs next to me with half-open eyes, "Hey, darlin'."

I snuggle back down next to him as he pulls me close. "We had another wonderful, but irresponsible, evening, young man," I reply.

"I personally thought it was very responsible. I took care of the woman I love. What more is there?"

We talk for a few minutes, but we don't have time to spare and hurriedly get up and dressed. This is my last chance to win *Next Real Star*.

Chapter Sixty-One – Julia

After our TV appearance and a few more interviews, I'm planning on meeting Raine for lunch. My family is still here, so we've planned to travel together to the arena. I'm getting my hair and makeup done in the hotel room, and then we'll all walk the red carpet to greet the media. This is a first, and I'm sure they're going to hammer us.

By the time we arrive at the arena, my whole body is shaking. This is it. At least Raine is here to prop me up. I fiercely clutch his hand as we get out of the car.

"Let's get 'em, hon," he whispers encouragingly as his eyes bore into mine.

I smile at his words, but my grip on his hand is still death-like. As we make our way onto the carpet toward the arena, cheers greet us warmly. I stop and wave at the fans lining the entrance, and then walk up to sign everything put in front of me.

I look back at Raine and he's not happy I'm doing this. He's glaring and scanning the crowd for anything unusual. He's always my protector, and tonight I'm grateful for it.

We reach the first media outlet and we're greeted warmly. The host asks to speak with both of us.

"We're back live, and we have Julia Tate and Raine Wagner here with us. I must say, you look stunning, Julia. Who are you wearing?" the host asks.

"Versace and Jimmy Choo shoes, and I'm sure Raine doesn't remember," I continue with a slight laugh. "He's in Giorgio Armani."

I look at Raine and smile as he shrugs his shoulders. He has no idea and frankly, doesn't care.

"There's been quite a bit of talk and excitement about you two these past few days. Besides Julia remaining on the show and the upcoming big tour, what's next for you both?"

Raine cuts in, pulling my hand up in the process. "We're also going to be a bit busy planning a wedding," he says, looking directly into the camera with a big smile, "October of this year."

The host exclaims, "Let me get a look at the ring ... oh my. Gorgeous! Wow ... you do have a lot going on! I know I'm excited, and I'm sure our viewers are equally thrilled for you both."

"Time to make it official and it couldn't be soon enough," Raine says firmly. Again, he's looking right at the camera, and I can't help but chuckle.

We make our way down the red carpet, stopping for pictures and brief interviews. For the most part, it goes well.

Then I have to go backstage as Raine and my family head to their seats. Raine will make sure he's sitting at the end of the row so he can, as quickly as possible, make it up on stage. I glance at him once as I walk into the backstage area, and he gives me a wink. Here we go.

Tonight, I'm singing first, thank God. After me, the order is Peter, Dewayne, and finally the favorite to win, Jeremy. Some famous artists will also perform, but we have no idea who they will be. Tonight, I'm actually looking forward to performing, and I remind myself to enjoy the night. This only happens once.

Katy announces the first celebrity performer, and the band Kingston takes the stage. As a huge fan of the group, I'm beside myself, but now I have to follow one of the biggest rock bands in the world. Great.

My celebrity producer, Reilley, walks up and gives me a big hug. "Are you ready?"

"Most definitely," I say, smiling.

Before I head out to sing, they show a clip of me meeting Reilley and working together. I walk behind a curtain and make my way to the microphone. I'll start to play as the curtain goes up. I look at the backing band and smile. For the first time since this whole craziness started, my fear escapes me. I'm ready. I've spent twenty-five years preparing for this moment.

As the curtain comes up and I start playing, the band follows along. It's a mid-tempo ballad, called *Bound by Song*, which tells of coming together late in life knowing you are bound together by something deeper than yourself. When I was making my way behind the curtain, Raine somehow found a way to make it up on stage and is standing next to me as the curtain rises.

I sing the first few lines, "Never wanted to do this life alone, but that was the path I was on, until you, until you. You filled my heart with hope and now I have a home. It's always been you, always you."

Raine steps to the mic and joins me in harmony and the audience is silent.

"We are bound by the love we made, bound by the love we gave, we are one—we are strong. Bound by the strength of two, found what was lost with you … we are Bound … by … Song." I sing solo, "Cause we are Bound by Song."

The crowd recovers from seeing Raine on stage with me, and during the musical interlude before the next verse, they respond enthusiastically. I smile at Raine as we sing the second verse together. I'm singing lead, and Raine sings the harmony part, and then we continue the chorus together, until the last chorus, which I sing solo as Raine looks at me, smiling.

The song ends and Raine leans in to kiss my cheek as the crowd goes nuts. He pulls me to him, and we look out at the audience, who are now on their feet. Even the two remaining judges, Brandi and Davis, are standing and clapping.

Katy approaches us and says, "Wow … what a beautiful surprise. Julia, did you write that song together?"

"We did, just yesterday."

"And we've heard you two will get married soon, any comment for our audience right now?"

I reply while Raine looks at me happily, "Just that these past few weeks have been the most amazing of my life. I've loved every minute that each of you," and here I gesture toward the crowd, "have given me to live this dream.

With our engagement, it's the icing on the cake. We couldn't be happier." As I speak, Raine pulls me to him. Katy nods at us as we both walk off the stage, hand in hand.

Katy continues, "There you have it, another surprise from Julia. We'll be back in a few minutes with our next performer."

My feet hardly touch the ground. I did it! I expected the show's staff to be upset, but they seem happy and smile at us. It's all about ratings, and our performance will help with that. We enter the green room, and two male contestants clap warmly. Peter has already headed toward the stage, but Jeremy and Dewayne each give Raine a fist-bump.

Raine sits down next to me and just looks at me. "Pure magic. We need to sing together more often," he says as he leans down to kiss my hand, which is still tightly enclosed in his.

"Definitely. The most amazing moment I've ever had on stage by far."

"Really? Even better than Andy Mitchell and Flashback 40? I'm shocked," he teases, and I laugh as I lean my head against his shoulder. "I guess I should let you finish the show, and I'll head back to my seat. That is, if they'll let me sit in the audience."

"All right, babe. I'll see you when we're done."

Raine leans down and kisses the top of my head. "I've been avoiding your lips so I won't mess up your makeup," he says mischievously.

"Well, I'm expecting you to mess it up later."

"I promise to."

##

I could literally pinch myself. What an amazing last performance show, but is it enough for me to win?

After the next celebrity performer, Peter performs a traditional big band style song. Peter moves effortlessly, and the girls scream. He makes big band look cool. Dewayne's performance has everyone on their feet, and then it's Jeremy's turn. Jeremy sits solo at the piano and performs a heartfelt number. Many of the young girls in the audience openly cry as I watch backstage, holding my breath. Jeremy's amazing and likely impossible to beat. He has the crowd in the palm of his hand.

At the end of the night, all the contestants and our celebrity producers gather on the stage. I stand next to Reilley, and it's one of the highlights of this whole experience. It's a breathless moment as the crowd is on their feet and confetti rains down on us. In each of our own ways, we won the night.

Backstage is filled with many laughs and a few tears as all twenty of us come back together. The next time we see each other, the winner will be revealed. This has been an experience I'll never forget.

Raine walks up to me and picks me up in a bear hug as my family follows close behind. We all pick up glasses of champagne, but it's my dad who speaks first, "To my daughter, Julia, one of the most talented and hard-working people I've ever known." I stand teary-eyed, leaning heavily against the love of my life. What an amazing night.

I'm relaxing with Raine in my hotel room, happy to enjoy the moment. After the show, Raine set up a big dinner so we could all celebrate together.

I'm stretched out along Raine's side, leaning against him heavily, exhaustion overcoming me. As I replay the events of the night in my mind, I ask. "Do you think it was enough to win ... honestly?"

His arm that's draped over my shoulder, pulls me tighter. "Hon, it was very good. You have a real shot. Jeremy's performance was excellent, I won't lie, and his fans will vote in droves. I really don't know how it will turn out, but you should be proud of yourself."

"I am ... it's just my competitive nature. I want to win. I can't help it. But I'll be happy no matter what."

He turns toward me as I nestle against the pillows, "I know of one way to make you even happier."

"I'm listening," I say, giving him my best "show me what you've got" smirk.

We don't say another word as our lips join. Although I'm exhausted, Raine can light a fuse of desire deep inside that I hope will never go out. My lips part as he rolls above me, determination in his eyes.

Chapter Sixty-Two – Julia

For the following weekend, we don't have anything to do before the final show reveal, so Raine and I get to enjoy the pool and the California scenery, and spend time with our family and friends. The pressure is off. No more performances, at least not in the immediate future. I didn't realize how much I need the down time, but by Monday, it all comes into focus. The big decision is tonight and finally, I'll know if I've won *Next Real Star*.

I'm anxious, but I'm filled with a deep calm knowing exactly who I am, and that I'm exactly where I should be in life. I'm standing in the bathroom and as I look at myself in the mirror, I casually run my hand over my stomach. No one knows yet but me. I haven't said anything to Raine. We've traveled down a very long and incredibly rough road, and ultimately, it's been perfect. Raine's voice brings me out of my daydream.

"What time do you need to get down there?" he asks.

"They're gonna have someone come up again to fix me up, and then we walk through the media line at five-thirty. Is Bret here?"

"Yep, and my parents should arrive soon. I didn't want them to miss this."

"Oh good … I wasn't sure who you'd arranged to join us. You kept me busy again last night," I say, laughing.

Raine walks into the bathroom and joins me, leaning against the door frame. "Just celebrating … speaking of celebrating, no matter what happens tonight, win or lose, it doesn't matter, big things are in store for you."

"I know … I had a call from a publishing company. They want to rep my songs."

Raine walks over and puts his arms around me, "And that's just the

183

beginning."

##

Later, we make our way to the arena with our entire group in tow. Again, we both answer media questions, but I'm so much more at ease. Whatever happens is out of my hands.

As the show starts, Raine joins me backstage. Katy comes out and sets up the evening.

"We've got a great show as we narrow it down to the winner," she says before pausing to continue, "I know everyone can't wait to find out if it will be Peter Robinson," and they play Peter's highlight reel, followed by segments about Dewayne, then me, and finally Jeremy. At the end of all four segments, we walk out as a group and the crowd explodes.

As we walk off stage, we're surprised by the first celebrity performer, and it's a doozy. Miles Stewart, one of the last surviving members of the biggest U.K. band ever, comes out and sings a medley of his greatest hits, backed by a full orchestra. Talk about surreal. I squeeze Raine's hand and glance at him. He gives me a toothy grin, clearly enjoying the night as much as me.

Then it's time to get to business. They'll cut the field down to the final two and then announce the winner. As Katy comes back on the air, we take center stage. At this point, I am rethinking my four-inch platforms. I'm shakier than I expected.

Katy turns to the camera as she says, "You, the voting public, have narrowed the field down to the final two, but before we get to it, let's get a word from the judges on their choices."

Davis and Brandi join in with their favorites. I receive praise for my songs, but Jeremy is the vocal favorite. I look at Raine during the commercial break and he gives me a reassuring smile.

As we come back from break, Katy relays what each of us will get at the conclusion of the show, and what the lucky winner gets. In addition to prizes from the sponsors, the winner receives five hundred thousand dollars. The winner is not tied to any specific contract, label, or record deal.

It's time for the show to cut the contestants down to two. Katy looks into the camera as my world stops. "Again, a record number of votes came in over the weekend. More than sixty-five million unique votes were recorded. But enough talk, let's get down to the results." Katy opens a sealed envelope. "The first performer leaving the show is … Dewayne Johnson."

The camera flashes to Dewayne as the crowd cheers for him loudly. Dewayne takes it well. He already has major labels after him.

The three of us remaining draw in closer. I'm standing between Peter and Jeremy.

Katy announces, "And now, we'll cut it down to two. The separation of votes between our final three was remarkably close." Katy opens a second sealed envelope and pauses for a moment. "The next performer leaving the show is … Peter Robinson."

Peter handles it like a pro and walks off the stage waving to his adoring fans. I hug Jeremy as the two of us take center stage. The crowd's going nuts. I'm overwhelmed by the support from the crowd. Jeremy has the young girls screaming, but I'm holding my own.

"There you have it," Katy continues, turning toward one of the cameras. We'll be back shortly with one more surprise … and then the new winner of *Next Real Star* will be revealed!"

The show goes to break, and I'm immediately escorted offstage to hair and makeup.

Chapter Sixty-Three – Raine and Julia

I'm standing next to Julia, watching like the proud fiancé I am. My phone buzzes. A text from Bret, of course.

'I think she's going to win.'

I text back, 'Don't jinx this shit.'

'Easy killer … just sayin'. Bet a game of golf on it?'

'Nope. We're both backing the same horse. Got to run.'

The cameras come back on as the next guest performer walks out singing acapella. It's Mariel singing her latest U.K. smash, and I have goose bumps because this woman can sing.

I walk over to Julia and put my arms around her. Julia leans against me hard. I swear I can feel her heart beating against my hands. Or maybe it's my heart about to come out of my chest. I want this for her more than anyone could possibly imagine.

##

I'm leaning against Raine and listening to Mariel, spellbound. What a voice. It causes me to doubt. I don't have a voice or anything like the power she does. Jeremy can sing like this, and so I'm resolved to the fact I'm the runner up, and that's okay. The five hundred thousand would have been a big help, though.

Mariel finishes, and Katy walks back out. They show a clip of Jeremy in his hometown greeting fans, and what life is like for him in Ohio. He's well-liked and a good kid with an amazing talent.

Next is my segment, and as it opens, Raine's face hits the big screen. His words bring me to tears. "I have never met anyone like her, and I've put her through so much. Too much, and she stood strong. The past few weeks have been magical for both of us, and I can't wait for the next chapter in our lives."

Raine's segment is followed by my dad showing the camera crew around my hometown in Nebraska, and then several bars holding "Julia Tate Fan Nights" during the show. I can't hold back the tears realizing so many people have helped me get to this place.

Then Katy turns to the camera and says, "I think we've all seen enough. Both are amazing writers and performers, and we would be proud to call them the winner of *Next Real Star*. Jeremy, Julia, please come out here on stage."

I grab Jeremy's hand and we walk out to join Katy.

##

As I stand on the side of the stage waiting for Julia's results, I never knew my chest could feel so tight. My phone buzzes. I pull the phone out of my pocket. Again, it's Bret.

'What did I tell you? You've got to breathe, man.'

I take a deep breath and look back out toward the stage. Julia looks so tiny. All I want to do is run out and protect her from this outcome.

Katy turns directly into a camera and says, "Again, after a record number of email and text votes, we have a winner."

The room is silent. The TV cameras flash to Davis and Brandi, taking it all in. Brandi's hands are up to her face as she waits anxiously. Davis sits stoically. Time has stopped.

##

I'm standing center-stage next to Jeremy, and my legs are shaking uncontrollably.

Katy continues to read the teleprompter, "It was so close, our accounting department verified the data more than five times." A man in a suit walks out and hands her an envelope. "And the winner, receiving the most first place votes is …"

I grip Jeremy's hand tightly, barely breathing.

Katy finally exclaims, "Julia Tate!"

My legs buckle as my hand comes to my mouth. I stare stunned at the camera. I'm too shocked to cry or move but I can hear the faint sound of applause in my ringing ears. I glance out to where my family is sitting, and they are going nuts. Then I turn to the side of the stage, scanning every face for Raine's and he's not there.

Katy walks toward me with a microphone and puts it up to my mouth, "I'm in complete and utter shock … I never … I didn't think. Jeremy is amazing, and what a voice. I really didn't think I was going to win."

Davis and Brandi, and the entire audience, are on their feet as confetti rains down on everyone.

I then ask into the microphone, "Where's Raine? Where is he?"

##

A stagehand is standing over me. "Man … man … are you okay?"

I dropped to my knees on the side of the stage. The suspense was too much, and I was holding my breath. I almost passed out. Bret was right.

"She won … Julia won," the stagehand yells in my ear. I must look dazed as I look up at him, grasping his hand and trying to stand.

##

I'm searching for Raine, and I finally find him. I watch as several stagehands are helping him up. My eyes meet his as he staggers toward me, arms wide as I run and fling myself in his arms.

"You did it, babe," he whispers in my ear. "You did it!"

"I won the night we had dinner in your room," I whisper back.

Raine then kisses me hard, again, on national television, and the audience, and especially the show's producers, love it. For the first time in a long time, a female contestant has won a reality talent show. Yes, I did it for myself, but also for all women. With Raine by my side. I have finally, really won.

END

Epilogue – Julia

After the show, Raine and I have a few days with no real commitments, so we decide to head out of town for a bit of a break. Raine has booked a flight for us up to San Francisco, and from there, we'll drive up to Napa for the weekend. Just the two of us.

As we are getting into our waiting car, headed toward the airport, Raine casually turns toward me and says, "I do have one little surprise."

"Yes," I say turning toward him, kissing him sloppily on the cheek.

"You'll see …"

"Oh … you're terrible! Just tell me."

Raine sits back and smiles. One of my hands is in his, and he's tracing a pattern on the inside of my hand. The slightest touch from him easily takes me over the edge, and my insides stir.

I pull my hand away. "No more until you tell me," I say, folding my arms across my chest in mock frustration.

He looks at me and laughs.

It doesn't take long to find out the surprise. Instead of taking a commercial flight, Raine arranged a private jet.

I get out of the car, overwhelmed. "Very cool."

"Keeps us away from the cameras and your fans. I want you to truly relax and enjoy yourself."

"This is why I love you so much," I say as I wrap one arm tight around his waist, and we walk toward the waiting jet.

As we take off, we watch the city that has changed my life slowly fade away. The ground is soon covered in green, and a majestic sun is shining down on the vineyards below. It's a short flight to Napa and a quick car ride to our resort. Raine has arranged everything. As soon as we are settled, we enjoy a delightful and much needed couple's massage in our room, followed by dinner.

##

I'm relaxing in the hot tub outside of our room as I look up at the enormous night sky. Raine slipped out of the room to take care of some business. Years earlier, I would have instantly been suspicious of his actions, but not anymore. I absentmindedly play with the engagement ring on my finger and wonder when I'll share my big news with him.

I called Jody earlier to let her know we'd arrived safely. So far, no one, not one paparazzi, has discovered us, which is amazing. I need this break and normalcy.

"I'm back, babe," Raine says from inside the room.

"Well, get your gorgeous ass in this hot tub," I yell back. I lean against the hot tub wall letting the bubbles soothe my aching shoulders.

"My, my ... ordering me around already."

"Comes with the territory."

Raine walks out smirking and replies, "Actually, I think I'm the one who marks my territory," and he quickly jumps into the hot tub, gathering me into his arms.

"Just like a dog," I say against his lips. "Got to lift your leg to claim what's yours."

And his head goes back as he laughs loudly, and then he plants a big kiss on my lips. The beauty of a personal hot tub is that I'm already naked. He pulls me on top of him and my head falls back as he leans in and kisses my neck hard.

We don't speak as I move on him. Raine keeps pulling me toward his eager lips, which can't seem to get enough. He lifts me out of the water, carrying me into the room, but we don't make it to the bed. He puts me down on the floor and continues making love to me.

He engulfs me, and as I'm about to have one of the best orgasms of my life, he grabs my free hand that is lying face up above my head, coming with me hard, yelling out as he does.

Finally, after several moments, I say, "I think our vacationing neighbors heard that one."

"I don't care. I couldn't help it," he says, rising to look at me. "I have one more surprise for you tomorrow."

"Oh, good lord! What is it?"

"My little secret."

"Ugh! You and your secrets," I tease. "Good," I say smiling up toward him. "I actually love surprises."

Raine quickly rolls over, gathers me in his still wet arms like I weigh nothing, and carefully walks to the bed as I wrap my arms around his neck. He lays me down and starts making love to me again. Who says libido starts to fade as you get older?

The next morning, we're enjoying a casual breakfast in our room, and thankfully I'm enjoying a cup of coffee. In a very good way, Raine kept me up most of the night. He's pacing around the room with this phone in his hand.

"Hon … the constant walking back and forth is making me dizzy," I say, smiling. This major tic never leaves him. He can't stay still, and I love this about him.

"Just making sure everything is set."

"Making sure what is set?" I ask, glancing up at him, one eyebrow raised.

A knock at the door interrupts us. I start to answer, but Raine beats me to it.

Odd, I think. What is up with him? And I soon find out. A lady walks in holding a large garment bag with Raine leading the way. I just sit dumbfounded at the table.

"Julia, my last surprise. With friends and family still so close by … I um … I thought," he stammers.

He looks toward the woman carrying the large bag for help, and she opens it up to reveal its contents. Out pours a white wedding gown and it's breathtaking.

191

Raine, clearly out of his element, is struggling as he gets the words out, "I know we said October, but what about today, at this gorgeous resort in this beautiful location? I don't want to wait one more day."

I'm stunned and stare at him blankly, with no time to respond.

Raine steps closer. "Let's get married here. I've called Bret and arranged everything with your family. My family is coming. What do you say?" Raine's brow crinkles with worry as he stares into my eyes.

I finally recover and nod as he leans in to kiss me.

My hands are trembling as I step into the foyer overlooking the winery. After my big surprise, Tracy and Jody both arrived within the hour. Everyone knew but me.

Raine has taken care of the marriage license; I have no idea how. I just had to sign it. The only thing that's missing is a ring for Raine. So, I called a local jeweler and picked something out for him over the phone. It's not perfect, but the platinum band looks good on his hand, and it will do until I can get him something else in Nashville.

I take a step forward as music begins to play and my dad walks up to take my arm. Right now, my terror is coming from saying personal words to Raine in front of others, not because of what we're doing. I'd marry him anyplace, and at any time. He's the love I always dreamed about, and doubt is not entering my mind.

I round the corner and when I get my first look at Raine, an inner peace overcomes me. It's surreal and I'm sure to capture it in my mind. Raine arranged a string quartet to play the song we wrote together, "Bound by Song," as I walk down the aisle. As I take my steps toward him, it's hard to catch my breath.

Bret leans in and whispers something to Raine, but Raine's eyes have not left mine. His smile gets larger as I walk toward him. Everyone in the room fades from view with each step. Finally, my dad is standing just a few feet from Raine. He lifts my hand toward Raine's, and it visibly shakes.

Raine leans toward me and whispers, "Are you sure?"

I look at him and smile, giving his hand a firm squeeze.

As the minister speaks, I give my flowers to Jody. Tracy, who is standing next to her, has tears streaming down her face, and I about lose it, but I'm determined to get through the most important words in my life without crying uncontrollably. Even though we're both writers, when it came to our vows, we're keeping it traditional.

"I, Raine, take you, Julia. To have and to hold, for better or worse, in sickness and in health, for richer or poorer, to love and to cherish, as long as we both shall live."

I repeat the same lines, firmly grasping his hands. When I look at his face, I don't think he's ever looked more handsome, or happier.

We finish our vows and Raine surprises me again with a black and white diamond wedding band to match my engagement ring.

As he leans in to kiss me, Bret yells out, "We've all already seen the big kiss on national television, man. Let's get this over with!"

Raine turns toward his good friend and scowls, and then he grabs me, laying a huge, passionate kiss on my lips. We're lip-locked for several seconds as everyone claps and cheers. Finally, he lets me up for air, and I'm sure my face is beet red. I'm not one for big public displays, but we've blown that out of the water.

I whisper in his ear, my eyes dancing, "Wait until your surprise later tonight."

"I love surprises, and I love you, darlin', with every ounce of my being."

And he lays another one on me in front of our small group of family and friends.

Although Raine arranged a wedding ceremony at the height of tourist season in Napa, the resort was able to come up with a private reception area for us. The good thing about the quick nuptials is that no photographers or reporters found out. The last-minute arrangements were a good decision, and we were able to maintain our privacy.

As we slow dance at the reception, we're oblivious to anyone around us. I wanted to leave immediately and go back to our own room, but we play the dutiful hosts and stay around for a bit.

Later, Tracy has a moment alone with me.

"You got it. The happy ending you've always deserved," she says, leaning in to give me a big hug.

"Thanks, girlfriend," I say with a huge smile. "Who would have thought this would have happened after so many years? What a ride."

Tracy holds up a glass of champagne toward me, "Cheers to my best friend, and your happy ending."

We clink glasses and it's at this moment that Tracy notices I'm drinking water.

"No champagne? Wait … why no champagne?"

I pause, looking down.

Recognition appears on Tracy's face. "Does he know? Is this why you got married so quickly? Oh wow!" A grin spreads across her face.

"No … and shush, that's not why. But I want to surprise him. I've been able to hide any champagne he's given me today and he hasn't noticed a thing. I just found out. It's early, Tracy, but I'm fairly sure. I'm never late."

"Wow … you are having a good year!"

"No kidding … Raine, the show, marriage, and now a baby. It's almost too much for one person. No one gets all of this."

"Hush! Yes, they do. I'm so happy for you."

We hug again right as Raine walks up to break up our party. He picks me up and waves goodbye to our guests still enjoying the reception. We ignore the obvious catcalls and cheers. He doesn't say a word as he whisks me down the hallway.

"You know, you could put me down now," I tease as he continues to walk boldly down the hall as if I am light as a feather.

"Nope. Tradition. I'll carry you over the threshold."

I relax my head against his shoulder, taking a moment to breathe him in. I look at him wondering if I'll always feel this much love for him.

Raine looks down at me. "What?"

"Just that I love you. That's all."

He kisses me hard while still walking. As we reach our room, he somehow manages to maneuver the key from his pocket to open the door, never letting my feet hit the ground.

He walks in, kicks the door closed behind him, and then he runs toward the bed, lightly flinging me on top of the covers. He reaches up and starts yanking at his tie and pulling his shirt over his head, stripping as quickly as possible. I cannot get out of my dress alone, so I just watch him, laughing and enjoying the show.

"I'm gonna need you to help me," I say. "I'm strapped into this dress, and I can't get out."

Raine stops his strip tease and comes to my aid. He turns me around as I lie on the bed and he starts to unbutton the many tiny buttons that begin at my upper back and reach down to the top of my ass, his lips following his fingers. I moan with each touch of his lips on my skin. When finished, he turns me around and slips the gown off my shoulders. I had time to get nice white, lacy lingerie and a tiny corset pushes up my breasts, accentuating my still small waist. He looks down and stops for a moment.

"Damn ... you look good."

I lean in and grab him behind the neck, slipping my shoes off one by one as I pull him down on top of me. We manage to keep our lips together as we struggle to free ourselves from our remaining, binding clothes. He leans around me and unfastens my corset and as it comes free, he plunges his head to my stomach, kissing me lingeringly.

Raine stops to look at me as he says, "I noticed you didn't drink any champagne tonight."

I take a quick breath.

"How long?" His lips continue to graze my skin tenderly and his hands follow with the lightest of touches as I shiver with his touch.

"Two, maybe three weeks tops. Probably happened that first night we made love without a condom. A lucky strike," I say, my eyes dancing as I watch his reaction. "You've guessed my surprise. We can't tell anyone, it's too soon."

He moves up to be face to face with me. "Our secret, but as soon as it's safe,

I'm buying a full-page ad in the *New York Times*," he says with all seriousness, and I giggle at him. He continues, the words choking him up, "I can't tell you what this means … to … me …"

"Oh yes … I think I can."

And his lips find mine and we hold on tight to each other with a sweet tenderness and profound love of knowing the gift that binds us together, tighter than we've ever dreamed possible. I'm carrying his child.

##

I spend the next few weeks making appearances on every show you can think of as the winner of *Next Real Star*. Raine makes a few appearances with me, and we officially announce our marriage. The outpouring of love is amazing. We haven't told anyone about the baby yet. Too soon. But I'll begin to show in a few months, and we'll have to tell the world.

Finally, we head back to Nashville to build our life together. I packed up my things and moved into Raine's house, but he's been looking for a bigger place with a master bedroom with a nursery attached.

I've been busy writing and preparing for the *Next Real Star* tour. The final four contestants are the show's main performers, but we'll be joined by the other sixteen contestants at different points, and many celebrity guests. I now have other artists recording a few of my songs, and my writing is in demand. I also started working on my own recording project. Everything is crazy busy, and I love it.

By the time I go on tour, I'll be very pregnant. We'll have to deal with that as it comes. Luckily, it's a short tour.

One afternoon, I'm sitting in my new office, talking to Tracy, who is now my assistant.

"Do you think you'll ever get used to all of this?" Tracy asks.

"Never," I reply. "But I'll take it. Can you believe I'm married to Raine, pregnant, working as a recording artist, and a songwriter? With everything that man and I went through. I still pinch myself sometimes."

"I hear you. And lucky me, I get to work with you," she says.

"That's the icing."

"I'm still waiting on one little thing though."

"And what is that, my friend?"

"My Andy Mitchell autograph … I'm still waiting," she says with all seriousness.

And I throw my head back and laugh as Tracy joins in.

Born by Song

The music continues ...

The second book in the Julia Tate Song Series by J. D. Williams.

Chapter One – Raine and Julia

I'm careening through the streets of Nashville at record speed. I've already called the hospital, and as I glance down at my beautiful wife, her face contorted in pain, it nearly destroys me. It's too soon. The baby is coming too soon.

"It's okay, love," I manage to get out, my constricted voice betraying the fear consuming my body. "Just hold on. We'll be there in a few minutes."

Julia groans, her head thrown back against the top of the car seat. Her eyes are shut from the pain.

I gun the engine even harder as we take the on ramp and my tires scream toward the hospital. Why did we move to the country? I should have life-flighted her to the hospital. My mind is racing and I'm silently pleading with God to get us there on time. She's barely six months pregnant with our child. It's just too soon.

I'm trying to keep it together, but the cramping in my abdomen is unlike anything I've ever experienced. Waves of pain sear through me, but I can't let Raine know how bad it is. I'm losing our baby with every second, and my heart constricts so hard I think it will explode from my chest.

I look up at Raine, purposefully avoiding the blanket wrapped around my waist. It's warm and wet, and I can't bear to look down. Raine's brow is deeply furrowed as he tries to maneuver down the street. I've never seen him look this stressed or frightened.

"Hon … don't worry. It'll be okay," I say as I drop my limp hand on his leg.

Without looking away from the road, Raine puts his hand on top of mine. It's so warm and comforting. I'm trying to stay focused, but all I want to do is sleep, so I close my eyes.

"Julia … Julia!" Raine yells at me and my eyes flash open. I blink quickly trying to stay awake.

He yells, "Stay with me!"

I manage to croak out, "I'm here. I promise. I'm here."

But I'm already feeling the loss. I've lost our baby.

When I finally pull up to the emergency room entrance, several staff members are waiting outside for us. After I had called the hospital, I called Julia's best friend, Tracy, and she's standing there as well.

Our car screeches to a stop as several people run to us. I had told them to look for a black Jaguar.

When I touched Julia's hand, it was ice cold. I'm doing my best to keep my fear in check.

As the staff starts to help Julia out of her car door, I jump out and run to her side. She passes out. As they pull her limp frame onto a gurney, I look down at the blanket lying on the car seat. I've never seen so much blood in my life.

"Raine … Raine! I've got the car," Tracy yells at me as she grabs the keys from my frozen hands and pushes me toward the building. My heavy legs struggle to follow as they rush Julia inside.

Nurses wheel Julia through double doors into a room as I stagger behind. The emergency team quickly puts an IV in her arm and yells to get a fetal heart monitor. The hospital has called our obstetrician, and Dr. Henley is on her way. I watch helplessly as they plug Julia into machines and listen to the monitor on her stomach, trying to find a heartbeat. My eyes glass over. There's no sound coming from the machine. How my heart aches to hear the tiny heartbeat I've heard so many times, but there's nothing.

Our doctor finally arrives and catches my eyes as I stand in the doorway. She grimaces. We're in good hands with Dr. Henley. She's one of the best.

I look at Julia lying there. She's so still and slightly blue, which shocks the hell out of me. But her monitor is beeping out her heartbeat. At least Julia has a heartbeat.

About J. D. Williams

J.D. Williams grew up in Nebraska, and after graduating from the University of NE – Lincoln, she moved to Minneapolis and toured with a pop cover band. As a recording artist and songwriter, she worked with some of the most talented artists, producers, and managers in the Minneapolis music scene. She has been involved in movie and video production and helped recording artists and bands as a manager and publicist. She is also an award-winning writer for general consumer and business publications and has had work printed in various national and regional publications.

Now living in Franklin, Tennessee, J.D. continues to write music, and her songs are featured in the Julia Tate Song Series of books.

For more information, go to **www.jdwilliamsbooks.com**

Follow on Facebook @jdwilliamsmusic

Follow on Instagram @jdwilliamsbooksofficial

Follow on Instagram @jdwilliamsmusicofficial

Start Over Again

https://li.sten.to/startoveragain

Verse 1
What to do, when a liar, he takes hold of you
He leaves your heart a mess
And your left wondering
Was it ever real, how he made you feel?
And then you realize, in his pack of lies
He gave you nothing, oh nothing

Chorus
Nothing but heartache
Nothing but white noise
You were a little toy, he brought out sometimes
There was no real with this boy
You forgive yourself, and take a good hard left
Trying to forget all those whispered lies ringing in your head
And just start over again

Verse 2
Where do you go, when all is said and done?
Picking up the pieces of your shattered soul, all alone
You can't help yourself, oh it seemed so real
You finally understand how this simple man had no heart to feel

And then you realize, in his pack of lies
He gave you nothing, oh nothing

Chorus
    Nothing but heartache
    Nothing but white noise
    You were a little toy, he brought out sometimes
    There was no real with this boy
    You forgive yourself, and take a good hard left
    Trying to forget all those whispered lies ringing in your head
    And just start over again

Bridge
    He made it look easy, as he walked away
    It was black and white
    While you see nothing
    Nothing but gray

Chorus
    Nothing but heartache
    Nothing but white noise
    You were a little toy, he brought out sometimes
    There was no real with this boy
    You forgive yourself, and take a good hard left
    Trying to forget all those whispered lies ringing in your head
    And just start over again
    Oh, and just start over again

Won't be a Tomorrow

https://jdwilliams.lsnto.me/wontbeatomorrow

Verse 1
    Your fingers running through my hair
    One last look from the top of the stairs
    It's one last text, one last call
    'Fore you lose it all …
    Like a lone gunman staring you down
    'Cept no one cares and there ain't a crowd
    You're standing still – and could lose it all
    With a single blow

Chorus
    The ends harder than you think
    Comes on stronger than you know
    Goodbye rushes toward you
    There won't be a tomorrow

Verse 2
    His fingers flexing round that gun
    Who will draw and who will run?
    How do you know when to risk it all?
    Or when to take a fall …
    It's one last kiss, one last night
    It takes your wind and part of your mind

You drew first – straight to my heart
That's the end of the show

Chorus (repeats)

Tag
   The ends harder than you think
   Comes on stronger than you know
   Goodbye rushes toward you
   There won't be a tomorrow